Roddy Murray

The Treasure

Hunters

Roddy Murray

© Roddy Murray 2014

Roddy Murray asserts the moral right to be identified as the author of this work.

Acknowledgements

I would like to thank Sandy Murray and Margaret Rustad for their assistance with proof reading and other invaluable suggestions. As ever, a big thank you to my mother Margaret Murray and my children Sebastien, Camille and Elliot for their encouragement. Finally a special thank you to Pauline MacGillivray.

By the same author;

Body and Soul

George Milne – Cat Detective

George Milne – Murder at the Butler's Convention

A Snow White Scenario

For my parents and for my children.

The Treasure Hunters

Chapter 1

Legoland

Jennifer Allerdyce sat in her office in Legoland, as so many of her colleagues insisted on calling MI6 headquarters, overlooking the Thames. She preferred to think about it as Babylon on Thames, resembling as it did a Babylonian Ziggurat. The architecture of her surroundings was not at the fore front of her mind today. It was, instead, focused on the impending meeting at 11 o'clock. She hated having to go cap in hand to the CIA for funds when HM Government couldn't or wouldn't fund something it had publically bragged about doing. She found herself yet again needing money from her opposite number in Langley. It was rarely a problem for them to come up with the readies. Their personnel promotion seemed to be based on how much money they could spend, irrespective of results. Maybe it actually was, she mused. The difficulty was more the fact that the Americans always wanted to put a US spin on any British operation if they were picking up the tab. That could be anything from full credit when things went really well to Britain taking the blame whenever they didn't. In her role as the senior liaison figure between the intelligence services of the two countries she had become acutely aware of the occasions when Britain had had to carry the can during her watch. On balance there had, however, been more successes than failures, which left her ambition to be the first woman to head MI6 alive. MI5 had seen fit to promote two women so far to the top job, which struck Jennifer as a little bit selfish of them. As far as MI6 was concerned she was the best chance for her gender to break through the glass ceiling so far. The more successes she could be associated with, the better her chances would be.

Over the years she had often worked with her American counterparts, and after initially thinking that Britain and the USA had nothing in common except a version of the same language she had come to realise that the Americans were very effective at what they did. For political reasons she had to work with them anyway but she had acquired a grudging respect for how they used their spending power to achieve results. On the occasions the aims and anticipated results of the CIA and HM Government coincided, they had proved very useful allies to have. She had worked in field operations during most of her early career and had met many US counterparts she admired. Unfortunately her opposite number at this particular moment in time, Brad Dexter, was an obnoxious shit she could have lived without.

Brad arrived and was shown into Jennifer's room exactly 10 minutes after the agreed appointment time, suggesting he was making the point that she needed his help but he didn't necessarily need hers.

"Jennifer," he oozed as he walked over and kissed her on both cheeks, as if he was French and she could stand his touch. "You're looking good, sweetheart. How can we colonials help you this time?"

He knew why he was there and she knew that he knew why he was there, but he wanted her to say it. To beg as it were.

"Thanks for coming, Brad," she said without any emotion. "You'll gather I need your cheque book again."

"Oh, and I was hoping for a hot date," he replied with a smile.

"As you know," Jennifer began, cutting straight to the chase. "Our lords and masters have publicly agreed to help the Syrian rebels fight off their tyrannical leaders etc. etc. and on this side of the pond that is officially limited to teaching them to use radios to better communicate. As you also know most of them are students or shopkeepers who have never fired a gun and therefore we have had to extend our training to include the basics: shooting skills primarily. The usual mission creep has kicked in and we have been asked, though in a very deniable way, to teach them how to use anti-tank weapons and anti-aircraft missiles. As a result, we now have a cadre of 30 Syrians in Northern England learning all this from instructors from Shh, you know who."

"You could tell me but you'd have to kill me," joked Brad.

For a split second Jennifer considered who she currently had available for that task but then refocused on the matter in hand.

"I believe it has been agreed that your government will provide the hardware and we will train them on UK soil. Unfortunately no funding has been forthcoming either for the Syrians' costs or for the trainers who temporarily are off the books of any official organisation. As a result we need raw cash and need it quickly."

"How much, and what currencies?" Brad asked focusing on business now that the initial banter had been dispensed with.

"Three million dollars and two million sterling," replied Jennifer without batting an eyelid. "That should let us square up with all concerned till the job is finished."

"Not a problem in principle," assured Brad. "But what is in it for us?"

"I assumed you would arrive with details of exactly what you would like in return."

"You know me so well. Okay. We want two of our guys involved in the training and we want everyone trained in the use of OUR hardware. Naturally the two guys we send will not exist, and will have a guaranteed escape route should anything turn nasty or public, including immunity from all law enforcement agencies within the United Kingdom."

"Agreed," confirmed Jennifer. The world was now full of American advisers who didn't exist and their bosses would always ensure a safe return to the States whatever political pressure might be brought to bear. Not just the traditional CIA types she was used to working with in her younger days in the field but now a whole range of Joint Special Operations Command personnel who had proliferated since 9/11. JSOC seemed to have taken the lead over the CIA under the present administration when it came to dodgy dealings overseas, and she increasingly found them calling the shots - often literally.

"We also want to supply all weaponry when the students return to their own country."

"Agreed. We have already started training them to use US small arms." So far the requests had been much as expected and well within her frame of reference. That suggested the big favour was still to come.

"Finally we want six genuine UK passports in names which I will provide at a later date, and four matching UK driving licences registered at your DVLA." For the first time Brad looked a little bit edgy at this last request.

"You know that's a non-starter," said Jennifer. "I don't have the clout for that and those above me wouldn't agree. Everyone's still a bit prickly about Israel using a fake British passport for their assassination in Dubai. Even if it was for your family to visit Disneyland Paris and you could personally guarantee it, you still wouldn't get them. Anyway, why don't you just make them yourselves; you usually do."

"We need these to be the real McCoy. Don't ask me why; it's classified way above me."

Jennifer stared at Brad in surprise. It was most unlike him to admit being out of the loop on anything they discussed. Even on occasions when she knew he was bluffing he would hint at deeper knowledge of all and any American activities in Europe. Here he was admitting to something classified above his pay grade.

Interesting, she thought to herself, and at the same time very worrying.

"I can't promise anything other than that I will take your request upstairs."

"I need more than that even if it's not a yes here and now. I can give you the personal guarantee of the President of the United States that these documents will not be used in any adverse way, or as you and I would put it, for business purposes. "

Jennifer stared at him cautiously. If he was saying that with a straight face then he had been told personally by the President that these were a personal favour. What that involved she didn't have a clue, but if it was off-the-radar stuff to MI6, MI5 and the CIA it might just be legitimate.

"You realise we will be monitoring any use of such documents anywhere in the world and will reserve the right to shaft the CIA in the press if they are used in any publicly negative activity?"

"That's my girl. It is sounding a little bit more hopeful. You'll get the cash tomorrow evening anywhere in the UK you would like it to be delivered. No strings attached. In the meantime we would appreciate it if serious consideration can be given to our request. I have been assured that the documents will be used in circumstances which support British interests too."

"Don't count on anything yet, but thanks for the money. Here are the coordinates for delivery."

They shook hands in a rather formal way. Brad had long since realised that a kiss on each cheek was never going to happen with Jennifer at the end of an interview when she was ready for it, a fact which he genuinely regretted. He found her trim figure in those formal business suits irresistible.

Chapter 2

Lost Money

On the face of it the flight from Edinburgh Airport to the very north of England had seemed routine on paper when he read the order. Admittedly it was going to be a night flight but the helicopter had enough technology to make that easy enough. He had to drop off some cargo then fly on to Teesside Airport where the chopper would be returned by an Army Air Corps pilot who would know nothing of its previous movements. Barry Cole couldn't see any great problem. All being well he would be dropping off the hire car in Manchester and be home with his feet up before sunrise the following day.

When he arrived at the Military Movement centre at Edinburgh Airport things had begun to get more complicated. Two tough looking Americans who were clearly CIA had been added to the cargo to be delivered and they had each brought with them massive bags which they refused to be parted from. That meant they contained weapons of some kind, thought Barry. The total weight of all personnel and equipment was borderline in terms of what would be possible with the Gazelle helicopter provided. The weight was only part of the problem though. He could just about squeeze the Americans and their personal luggage inside the aircraft but there would be no room for the two large metal boxes which he had expected to be the only cargo.

Risking security he phoned his contact at MI6 in London and explained the problem. The answer didn't help much. "Improvise," he had been told before the phone went dead. "Thank you and goodnight," he thought to himself.

Improvising was something he was good at though.

"Have you guys got any HUSLE kit here?" he asked the duty movers, wondering if they had any Helicopter Underslung Load Equipment.

A thumbs-up confirmed that some could be obtained within 30 minutes and that one of the movers knew how to rig it.

"How long is this gonna take?" asked one of the Americans who looked jumpy, as if he was in downtown Mogadishu rather than the east of Scotland. "We don't have all night."

"As long as it takes to get these crates secured under the chopper. As far as I'm concerned you two are hitchhikers. My job is to deliver them, not you."

The nearest of the Americans looked at Barry with undisguised hostility but Barry ignored him and set to work checking the helicopter ready for the flight. Finding his best staring going unnoticed, the American sat on his bag and watched the activity around him with a still angry look on his face. His colleague had been sitting on his bag throughout the exchange and just looked bored.

The HUSLE equipment arrived and Barry and a switched-on corporal, who seemed destined to go further, soon got the crates into the nets ready to be secured to the undercarriage of the aircraft once it was in the air.

"Do you guys want your bags in here too?" he asked his passengers, knowing the answer.

"They stay with us," replied the bored agent.

When he was happy that everything was in order and after double checking that he would have sufficient fuel to complete the flight he turned to the two CIA agents.

"Right gents, your taxi is ready."

The movers watched with mild amusement as the two Americans struggled to get themselves and their luggage into the tight rear seats of the chopper. After what seemed an age they had somehow managed to squeeze themselves and their bags inside. With a hefty shove from the corporal the door was shut and Barry fired up the engine. He gently took off and hovered while the corporal checked the HUSLE and hitched it to the rigging on the helicopter itself. When he was sure all was safe, he gave the signal to Barry who gained height and headed south.

Barry hated flying with an underslung load on a mission like this. The helicopter handled like a brick and he had to constantly be aware of the danger of the load swinging about. Added to that was the fact that he was flying a forty foot high object rather than one that was only twelve foot high. All in all he couldn't wait to get to the drop off point and get rid of his passengers and cargo. This trip had turned from routine to pain in the neck too quickly for his liking. He flew high enough to clear Edinburgh safely then headed south, skirting round the Pentland Hills. He flew south as low as he dared with a weather eye on the fuel gauge. He had been more than happy with the quantity of fuel required for a solo trip to the military training area then on to Teesside Airport. Now he had two large American gentlemen and their equally large luggage which would drain the fuel far quicker. Added to this was the need to fly slowly, way slower than the optimum speed for economy. This all played on his mind and, more importantly, made him even more pissed off than he had been when he saw his unexpected passengers. Nonetheless he reckoned he could still make it all the way at a push. The trip would be a breeze as soon as he dropped off his load and guests.

To add to his bad mood the weather decided to give him a kick in the teeth too. The wind got up, making the handling of the helicopter even more difficult, and the rain came on and reduced his visibility to the point where he had to rely on his instruments and fly higher than he liked.

He looked up at an imaginary deity and mumbled: "Cheers mate !"

By the time he was approaching the border between Scotland and England he was angry at everyone and everything. He was also seriously struggling to control the helicopter and its load to the extent that his two passengers started to mumble critically about his flying abilities. Had they accurately gauged his mood and known his temperament they would have shown more restraint. As the wind and rain increased, the comments from the back became more critical and Barry's mood became less conducive to flying the helicopter safely to its destination. His concentration wavered slightly at first but he managed to re-focus. Then as the helicopter lurched sideways in a particularly strong gust of wind which started the underslung load swinging dangerously, he heard a voice behind say quite clearly, "this guy can't fly for shit."

Ignoring instruments, height, swinging load and all, Barry turned round and shouted over the noise of it all that anyone unhappy with his abilities could "get the fuck out of his helicopter and walk". In fact any more criticism from the cheap seats and he would personally kick them out.

At this the Americans became quiet. Not because they were afraid of Barry, but rather they were afraid of being in a storm, in a helicopter with a swaying load with the pilot looking backward at them and paying no attention to flying the aircraft. After staring at them to make sure they had got the message Barry turned back to the task of flying. However, by then it was too late to avoid the power lines looming out of the rain in front of them. Barry saw them at the last moment and although he tried to swerve to the side of the cables the load swung back and caught in the wires. With years of experience ruling his reflexes he somehow managed to keep the helicopter airborne and roughly still above the power lines.

"Bugger," was all he managed to say.

Experience kicked in however and he turned and shouted, "One of you needs to climb out and cut the rope on the underslung load."

"Fuck you," said the more talkative of the Americans.

"One of you has to or we are all fucked," Barry shouted back calmly.

Without saying a word the quieter of the Americans took a knife from his pocket and, bracing himself, opened the door on his side of the helicopter. It felt as if the powers of hell had been unleashed as the wind and rain swirled into the aircraft and Barry only just manage to keep it level at the end of its mooring rope. The American took a deep breath and eased himself out of the door with a struggle placing one foot then the other on to the landing sled. With surprising grace he managed to keep hold of the door and lower himself on the runner till he could reach under the helicopter. With a further movement he lowered himself till he was sitting on the runner and then he reached underneath and grabbed the nearest piece of the HUSLE. Although they could only see his shoulders the others could tell that he was sawing away at the rope. After a minute or two the helicopter lurched as one of the strands of rope was cut. The two observers in the helicopter braced themselves but Barry managed also to keep the aircraft steady. More sawing of rope followed and after five minutes another tie was cut, allowing the load to fall and the helicopter to free itself simultaneously.

The chatty American mouthed off that his buddy had saved their asses just a bit too loud for Barry, who was essentially certifiable from Post-Traumatic Stress Disorder at the best of times and homicidal/suicidal on a bad day. He had never sought help from any of the agencies who could have provided treatment or medication. As a result something deep within Barry snapped and as the chopper soared upward he removed his seatbelt, radio and headset. Initially balancing the main controls with his knees he turned and asked the CIA agent behind him if he had a problem.

The answer was an obvious "yes, and it's the pilot of this helicopter" but unfortunately the agent summarised it as "Fuck You".

Barry's blue touch paper had been lit and he launched himself into the rear of the helicopter swinging punches as he went. The American behind let his training kick-in and fought back.

Outside the helicopter the senior agent managed to pull himself upright on the landing sled and was pleased to sense the aircraft going upwards. He pulled himself further round against the wind and brought his feet to a point where they could support him on the runners.

Pushing himself upright with the last reserves of energy he steadied himself preparing to jump into his seat. At that point, however, he looked inside the aircraft and saw the pilot in the backseats fighting with his fellow CIA agent.

As a man of few words he restricted himself to mumbling "shit". Then he turned towards the front door of the helicopter with the intention of taking the controls. He had trained on helicopters, Blackhawk not Gazelles, but he reckoned if he could just get to the controls he could land it safely. He pulled and pushed with all his remaining strength till he was forward on the sled and could grab the door where the pilot would normally enter. His training allowed him to blank out the bloodbath in the rear of the helicopter.

With a supreme effort he managed to open the door against the wind and got himself through, grabbing hold of the controls just as the aircraft hit the ground and burst into flames. One or more of the three occupants might have survived if the flames had not quickly reached the bulky luggage carried by the Americans. Once it did, there was a huge fireball followed by the sound of bullets exploding in the heat and then a fireball of high explosives, which engulfed the wreckage of the helicopter.

Chapter 3

Figure at night

As a helicopter exploded in a valley of an army training area in Northern England, the inhabitants of Kirkton slept soundly in their beds. Not a hint of the sound of gunfire disturbed their slumber. The explosion of training munitions left them in peaceful oblivion. The flash of aviation fuel was too far away to awaken them and the sound of screams, the smell of burning flesh and the impressive arc through the air of an anti-aircraft missile launched at random into the skies above their heads had no effect.

Only one figure watched it. The figure had also watched a helicopter snag on electricity pylons before a hero from within had climbed out and cut the stricken aircraft free. The figure watched as the helicopter rose up and flew towards the training area to the south, disappearing behind the Cheviot Hills in the process. The figure had also seen something falling from underneath the helicopter before it broke free. Intrigued, the shadow had climbed the hill from the road towards the offending electricity mast to see if a body or something else had fallen. The climb was steep and took the breath away from the inquisitive figure. When it arrived beneath the scene of the earlier drama it took time to recover its breath. When it did though, it found two large metal containers, the size of pirate's chests, embedded in the ground below.

The chests were intact, although the impact had twisted the casing. The figure took a multitool from a coat pocket and, with considerable effort forced the catch on the first chest. As the lid flopped open a collection of vacuum-packed bundles of bank notes became visible. The second chest revealed a similar treasure. The figure viewed the contents with interest. Using the main blade from the multi-tool, the top bundle from each container was opened, allowing in the air and fate in equal measures. One bundle contained grubby, twenty pound notes while the other revealed rather crisp US dollars. The shadow stared in surprise and amazement at its find. It looked up, perhaps searching for a beneficent god, perhaps in guilt looking for the money's rightful owner, as if the helicopter might return. Averting its eyes from the gift-horse the figure started to drag the containers down the hill towards the awaiting car. The weight and the undergrowth made this a difficult task which took some three hours to complete. At the vehicle the figure again opened the containers and slowly but surely transferred the contents into the boot of the car.

Half way through this process a small red light became visible in each one. The shadowy figure stopped its greedy task and stared. A flicker of recognition registered on its face. So somebody was tracking these items.

The rest of the transfer was rushed but thorough. Not a single package was left behind. The figure paused when all the money had been transferred to the boot of the car. Now, it considered; how to throw the bloodhounds off the scent.

Chapter 4

Bobby Roberton heads South

Bobby Roberton had had a busy day. In fact he had had a busy week. He had been collecting and delivering cattle and sheep all over the Borders for 20 days now non-stop and he was shattered. He had one more trip to do before taking four days off and he couldn't wait. After a long-haul trip with sheep from the Borders to Yorkshire he was faced with a stark choice. He could attempt to sleep at his mother's house and put up with a constant stream of criticism of his choice of girlfriend. The alternative was to try to sleep at his girlfriend's house, which was actually her parent's house, and put up with a constant stream of criticism of his mother. The other standard option was to crash out at his friend Jack's flat which almost certainly entailed a vast quantity of alcohol and an illegal start to his driving the next day. After due consideration, he forwent the vague chance of sex with his girlfriend in the early hours and went for the safest option, sleeping in his cab, in a layby on the outskirts of Kirkton.

Unbeknownst to him this meant his truck provided the perfect hiding place for two metal containers with tracking devices which until recently had held £2 million and $3 million respectively. As he slept and dreamed of sheep, Yorkie bars and the open roads of England, a shadowy figure carefully placed two such containers in the lower level of his cattle truck.

Bobby awoke the next day having slept far better than he would have done elsewhere and headed off to York, oblivious to the fact that his every gear change was being monitored by both the CIA and MI6. He drove down the A1 heading for a full cooked breakfast at Scotch Corner, completely unaware that a unit of anti-terrorist police were en-route to intercept him at his first stop.

Just before Scotch Corner at Barton Truck Services, he stopped in the park beside the other trucks, got out and stretched, happy in the knowledge that he was on his way to four day's peace. As he did so he was struck behind the knees by an expert and as he collapsed on the ground found himself staring up the barrels of several weapons wielded by tough looking individuals in masks who tried to reassure all around them with shouts of "police, stop and we won't shoot".

A long period of frustration and embarrassment followed as anti-terrorist police, MI6 figures, MI5 personnel and the army bomb squad searched Bobby's truck. An early "Ahaa" from one of what had previously been Special Branches' finest when the containers were found, nestling amongst some sheep droppings, was reduced to a "shit" when the containers were found to be empty.

Bobby was threatened with laws and sanctions he had never heard of and suspected were unconnected to livestock transportation rules, before an intelligent looking woman in a very smart business suit called off the various thugs gathered around and walked up to him.

"Bobby," she said. "Do you know what these are?" And she pointed to the two metal containers which had been pulled from his truck.

"No idea," he replied honestly.

"Have you parked up and slept in your truck recently? Specifically last night?" she asked.

"Yes," replied Bobby half hypnotised by the attractive older woman who was questioning him and by the surreal nature of what was happening around. "I crashed out in a layby near Kirkton last night. It was easier than going home or to my girlfriend's house."

To his surprise the lady produced a tablet from her large handbag and pointed to a map.

"This layby?" she asked, pointing to a small scale map of Kirkton.

Bobby peered at it and recognised the layby straight away.

"Yep," he replied feeling as if he was making his way out of the woods.

"Thank you Mr Roberton," replied the woman, with a look of disappointment on her face. "You have been involved in an anti-terror exercise, designed to safeguard our livestock transportation infrastructure. I hope you have not been inconvenienced or alarmed. The Ministry of Transport appreciates your cooperation. For security reasons, please do not discuss the details of this exercise with anyone."

Bobby looked at the woman, who smiled a rather unnatural and scary smile. Whatever she may have looked like to him, he realised he was off the hook for whatever they had suspected him of doing and was free to continue with his journey. Apart from anything else he was hungry and a full cooked breakfast was only a hundred feet away

"No problem," he said cheerily. "Glad you are taking the transportation of sheep and cattle seriously. We don't really get the credit we deserve."

By then though, the woman had lost interest in him, livestock transportation and perhaps even the will to live.

He shut up, climbed into his cab and decided to eat at the next services he came to. Maybe there he could enjoy a full cooked breakfast without the heartburn associated with being a national security threat.

Chapter 5

Old Bill

Sgt William Borthwick had been born into a family of Scottish policemen. He was the third generation of his family to join the forces of law and order. His grandfather had been an old fashioned policeman in the days of 'a clip around the ear', when policemen who had to arrest people on their patch for minor offences had somehow failed. Bill Borthwick's father Bob had then followed into the family business as an old fashioned policeman from the start. He had plodded the beat in Edinburgh for years before moving to The Scottish Borders shortly before retiring. He had arrested plenty of people in Edinburgh, though very few in the Borders, and had even been awarded The Queen's Police Medal for meritorious service during the miner's strike shortly before retiring. At heart though, he was an old fashioned copper like his father and raised young William to be an old fashioned copper from a very early age.

Thus at the age of 22, after a stint in the army 'to see the world', William Borthwick joined the Police as an old fashioned copper, as had always been planned. His 'seeing the world' had consisted of one tour of Belfast at the height of the troubles and three years in Redford Barracks in Edinburgh. His school mates had seen more of the world on holiday in Spain and Greece. He had, however, seen life at the sharp end and always felt it had benefitted him in later life in a way that foreign holidays never could.

His father had wisely recommended that he join a force far from home and young Bill had therefore joined the Northern constabulary and been posted to Wick. Although a relatively small town it had more than its fair share of weekend battles which Belfast had more than prepared Bill for. As a result of that and his sheer size, he thrived in his new environment and found the relatively quiet lifestyle most of the week to his liking. After a few years he noticed a vacancy posted on the station notice board for 'Constable to the Outer Isles'. This was a three year commitment which involved the incumbent touring the islands and ensuring that the inhabitants weren't up to any serious mischief. Bill jumped at the chance and signed up for three years of tranquillity. The islands were remote enough that any trouble was anticipated well in advance and sorted by the locals themselves as a general rule. The booking system for his travel arrangements meant that each island knew weeks before that he was coming. As a result, all the untaxed vehicles were parked off public roads, pub opening hours were adhered to meticulously for the duration of his brief visit and any poaching or smuggling was delayed for a day or two. This meant that he was never required to arrest anyone during his time in office with the exception of one drunken tourist in Orkney who had unwisely punched him on the nose in front of the locals. Everyone was polite to him and knew him by name, even if he didn't initially know them from Adam. He enjoyed the posting so much that when his time was up and there were no takers to replace him he managed to extend his time by a further two years.

It was during this five year idyll that he met and fell for his wife Mary. They met at a fund raiser for the Life Boat Institute of which her father was the local coxswain. Bill bought some raffle tickets and their eyes had met. He later bought three more batches of raffle tickets from her and to no one's surprise won several of the prizes, including a bottle of 12-year-old Scapa Malt whisky. Mary had brought him the prizes each time. They had danced, although he was there in official capacity and wore his uniform. At the end of the night they went their separate ways with a date to meet for lunch the next day, which was a Sunday and Bill's day off. Love had blossomed and they had been married three months later in the church in Kirkwall where Mary's parents had wed.

Their marriage had been and had remained a happy one from day one. Bill stayed in The Northern Constabulary for twenty years before being seconded undercover to Lothian and Borders police. During his time there he impressed his bosses sufficiently to be offered promotion and a rural posting if he transferred forces at the end of a further stint undercover in Edinburgh. After discussions with Mary and much soul searching they decided to accept the offer. Returning to Kirkwall was not going to be possible while Bill was in uniform so it made sense to take the promotion on offer and thus boost his pension so that when he did eventually retire and they moved back there they would be considerably better off.

And so they had found themselves moving to the Scottish Borders and Bill had found himself in charge of the community police officers who covered all the small rural villages including Kirkton. He and his wife had fallen in love with the area and Mary found her rheumatism far less painful than it been in the Orkney winters.

Although Mary was not able to enjoy the outdoor activities as much as her husband, she loved the friendly welcome of all the village clubs and societies. She was, therefore an active member of the Woman's Rural, the village art group and the line dancing club when her health permitted.

For his part, Bill loved to walk, play golf, fish and shoot. Any activity, in fact, that allowed him to be outdoors and free. He would even stay in uniform when he returned to the village and plod the beat, by choice, despite the fact that a young and ambitious female Police Constable did the same duty three days per week. To allay her fears that Bill felt she wasn't up to the job, and to avoid any gender based legal action against him, Bill had early on plodded the beat in other villages too, along with the community constables assigned there. All this, he would say, was to put back three generations of experience gathered from his family's old fashioned coppering activity of walking the beat.

He had, however, confided in WPC Janice Mackay while walking the few streets of Kirkton and Little Kirkton that he missed this part of the job (he couldn't bring himself to think of her as anything but WPC rather than PC even if that was no longer considered PC). That, more than anything else was why he walked the streets of 'his patch'. After a while Janice relaxed about Old Bill's encroachment onto her turf and in a way felt slightly sorry for him. Promotion had taken away the part of the job he loved the most. He had missed the contact with local people and the reassurance that his sizeable presence brought. That was a good feeling which she herself felt on a regular basis. But then, perhaps also, he didn't want to go home too early each night. She couldn't be sure. Either way he was due for retirement soon and she was determined to rocket to the top of her chosen profession. That wasn't going to happen if she rocked the boat over something as trivial as unnecessary company on the beat. So she listened and learned, and bided her time. She did however notice that as the months until Bill's retirement shrank to weeks he became increasingly nervous to ensure that everything was left in order for whoever took his place. Little had been allowed to happen on his watch and he did not want any crimes or excitement tainting people's memories of him and his sterling service to peaceful village life.

Chapter 6

Kirkton

The village lay almost on the border with England but slightly on the Scottish side. It was more accurate to describe it as two villages, Kirkton and Little Kirkton which faced each other like ancient rivals across the Rowent Water. Kirkton was the bigger of the two by a factor of three or so and boasted the Wagon Hotel, 'The Village Shop', a garage with petrol sales, a post office and a hairdresser. Little Kirkton had less to boast about: just the Reiver Hotel sitting prominently on the edge of the village green. The population was a mix of long settled families, the comfortably retired who had blown in from the length and breadth of the United Kingdom, a few incomer families of working age and a lot of absentees who owned holiday homes. This eclectic mix provided sufficient custom to support the remaining businesses in Kirkton when assisted by tourists and the absentees during the summer season. The hotels also benefitted from the patronage of the shooting and fishing fraternity who regarded the area as having excellent sporting facilities and came with their chequebooks to slaughter suicidal pheasants and partridges by the hundred or to do battle with the wily salmon in the nearby river Tweed. Amongst those of working age, many worked on the land one way or another, as farmers or farm contractors, or by selling and maintaining the machinery required by modern farming methods. Others looked after the game which brought the shooters from the cities for their annual sport or learned the ways and hiding places of the salmon to share with the fishermen on boats on the Tweed or over a dram in the hotels afterwards.

The hotels and pubs in the Borders (neither Scottish nor English to most here) were often the meeting places of different nationalities, cultures and backgrounds where hard days outdoors were forgotten in good company. To this mix was added a selection of walkers from around the British Isles and the wider world. Kirkton was a walker's paradise if you enjoyed walking up and down hills in often miserable weather. Some were young and challenging themselves on the long North-South walks over a period of weeks. Some were older but attempting the same feat while they still could, ticking off another item on their bucket list. Others opted for the shorter and easier East-West walks which followed the rolling Border's landscape and wound through the sites of ancient abbeys and castles, on a pilgrimage of their own creation. Walkers shared the feeling of warmth and friendly banter in the pubs after a hard day's labour, but unlike their farming and sporting counterparts, those who had just completed the long range walks often looked as if their time outdoors hadn't done them any good at all.

In Kirkton the two hotels served as additional meeting facilities for many of the clubs and societies which were active in the twin villages. Committees would meet in the bars or restaurants by arrangement with staff and other clubs, and as a result many people who would otherwise never darken the doorstep of a public house could be found associating with hardened drinkers, a single dry sherry in their hand. This removal of boundaries and throwing together of a cross section of village society enhanced the friendly nature of the village in general, the exchange of ideas and the spread of gossip in particular.

Chapter 7

Treasure Hunting

It was a mild but damp December morning which, although cold, had not produced any frost. Farmers were out and about early feeding their animals and being thankful for the continuing mild spell. This allowed them to keep their beasts outdoors longer than normal, saving money on feedstuff and man hours. There was still some grazing to be had in the fields although they were very wet in the lower-lying areas. The forecast was for this weather to continue and for this Monday specifically to be rain free. All in all this provided sufficient incentive for those with good reason to get outdoors as early as possible to do so. These were in fact perfect conditions for metal detecting.

David Ramsay and Clive Armstrong were very keen detectorists. David had been active in the hobby for well over 10 years while Clive had started 18 months before but had soon caught up with David in terms of enthusiasm and ownership of equipment. Together they had spent hundreds of hours sweeping their machines over acres of farmland in the Scottish Borders and occasionally further afield.

David had accumulated a large collection of finds over the years including a number of very old hammered silver coins. Many of these he had submitted to the Treasure Trove Unit in Edinburgh, either receiving them back once recorded, or receiving a useful ex gratia payment. Any such payment had immediately been reinvested in additional equipment, to the extent that he now owned seven different detectors. As in many activities, impressive equipment compensated for any lack of achievement.

Clive had been invited to go along with David one day while the two men were sitting in the midst of a very noisy evening arranged by their wives to celebrate the birthday of David's nine year old daughter Chloe. A number of parents and friends were there, and what seemed like an impossible number of children aged from five to 18. The volume levels were very high throughout the evening and it was difficult to make yourself heard above it. The two husbands had not really known each other before the start of the event but had found themselves trying to keep out of the scene of carnage that was the buffet on the kitchen table by sitting as far from it as possible in the lounge. Having covered the usual polite topics of what each did for a living, their children's progress at school etc., there had been a pause. They had nothing obvious in common except wives who were friends but so far the conversation had not indicated to either of them that the other was to be avoided and so they persevered.

They had watched the children running to and fro when the cakes appeared for a while before David had restarted the conversation.

"Any hobbies on the go?" he had asked vaguely with little real interest.

"I used to do a fair bit of running till I twisted my knee out on the hills but not really found anything to take its place. It isn't easy when you're a permanent taxi service for the kids after work. You?"

It was then that David had mentioned metal detecting and some of the finds he had made. Clive surprised himself by really taking an interest and found himself also fancying giving it a go with a certain level of school boy enthusiasm. What if they found some gold or a hoard of ancient and valuable coins? Men never fully grow out of being little boys.

After a bit of discussion it was decided that the two men would meet up the following Saturday quite early, before the rest of their respective households had surfaced, and have a search about. The trip did not unearth any major gold or pirate treasure but a sufficient number of interesting objects to make it worthwhile. David was generous enough to allow Clive to use one of his best machines, complete with a wireless headset arrangement. After less than half an hour Clive heard a high pitched signal rather than the low tone he was learning meant iron junk of some kind. He dug with the little trowel he had brought form his wife's gardening implements and soon discovered a huge round coin. He picked it out of the earth in triumph and shouted to David with undisguised glee. David took his headphones off carefully and walked over. Wiping the soil from the coin he realised it was a badly worn 'Cartwheel Penny'. He explained to Clive that it was an experimental coin from 1797 made by steam press and that sufficient of them had been made that they were not hugely valuable, even in perfect condition. This one had been in the ground for so long and was almost smooth; so much so that it might be worth a few pounds at best.

Clive had listened to the first part of David's explanation and kept nodding even after he stopped listening to the details. To him it was his first real find. It was a coin; an ancient coin, worth pounds. It was treasure and he was hooked.

Chapter 8

The Missing Hoard

David and Clive had been out detecting together on numerous occasions since then and had found many things together. They had also been out separately sometimes and always showed each other any finds from the solo trips. In this way their friendship grew beyond the initial requirements to get on simply because their wives were friends. Whilst they could talk enthusiastically for hours on the subject other members of their families and their friends and colleagues had learned to flee or change the subject quickly to avoid an hour or so of unsolicited detail on their latest expeditions.

About a year or so after the first trip out together, David noticed that the local history society was having a talk from one of the people responsible for dealing with Treasure Trove finds in Scotland. He let Clive know and it was agreed that they would both attend and put a face to the person they had sent some of their finds to.

The History Society was one of the countless clubs and societies which thrived in Kirkton, and its membership consisted of people from a range of backgrounds who had an interest in the history of the area or history in general. When David and Clive walked into the village hall on the evening of the meeting they halved the average age of those attending, if you left out Dr Dorothy Pitches, the guest speaker who looked about twelve. Despite this they were both made very welcome and took their places in the middle of the audience.

Dorothy was introduced by the chairman who spoke confidently and well from years of public speaking but looked as if he may have lived through much of the history being discussed at the meetings. If his own knowledge didn't go back far enough, others present looked like they could fill in any gaps. There were some other younger, middle-aged figures present, but not many. It looked like in Kirkton, history belonged to the elderly.

This was clearly not the case in Edinburgh, if Dorothy (call me Dot) Pitches was anything to go by. Her talk was an enthusiastic, almost breathless, run through the many recent discoveries in Scotland and the Borders in particular, which were making historians rethink history. She was a huge fan of detectorists, as long as they informed her department of anything pre-1800 which they found. Most objects were handed back but the information provided by what and where objects had been unearthed was invaluable to her team.

Not all the members kept up with her as she emphasised the importance of sending digital photographs of objects by email to her with accurate GPS grids. They were, however, fascinated to see her photographs of recent finds in the area and reassured by her enthusiasm that the torch of safeguarding the country's heritage had now been placed in safe hands.

David and Clive found the talk very enjoyable and both basked in the occasional praise from Dot towards responsible detectorists who were assisting so much with her work. They were, however, both more interested in the various finds displayed on the slides she had brought with her. One in particular grabbed both their attention.

Dorothy had a slide of three hammered coins from the reign of William the Lion of Scotland, or William I as he was also known. He had reigned from 1165 till 1214 and spent most of that time failing to win back Northumbria from the English. After singlehandedly charging the English troops at the Battle of Alnwick in 1174, he was captured and locked up, eventually in France, until he signed the Treaty of Falaise. None of this particularly interested either David or Clive, nor the fact that Richard

the Lionheart had released Scotland from the treaty in
return for 10,000 marks in silver to help fund the third
crusade. No, their ears pricked up when Doctor Dot
revealed that some of this ransom had reputedly gone
missing in the Border area on its way to the English
coffers and had had to be replaced by the Scottish court.
Approximately 2,000 hammered silver coins with a value
of perhaps £100,000 had never been discovered. The
only reference was from an obscure text of 1293
credited to Thomas the Rhymer who mentioned that
part of the ransom had 'benn Hyd by Theiffes' and never
seen again. As Dot said, he was also known as good
Thomas because he never lied. The three coins had been
found in the Rowent valley in near perfect condition,
within a six foot radius of each other and could easily,
therefore, be part of a much larger hoard. They could
perhaps even be the King's ransom, 'Hyd by Theiffes'
and never seen again.

At this point she stopped and took questions. There
were many from the members, and she answered them
all, demonstrating an encyclopaedic knowledge of
Scottish history in the process. She dealt patiently with
the long-winded questions designed to demonstrate the
asker's knowledge rather than to test her own, and she
cheerfully accepted the invitation to stay for a cup of tea
and some home baking. This was largely because David
had spoken to her on the phone the day before and

promised to hand her some of his most recent finds to be evaluated, and she was aware of his earlier contributions to her work. After politely listening to a number of kind comments from members of the history society she made her way towards David and Clive who were loitering with intent at the back of the hall.

"Hello David," she said, "what have you found for me this time?"

"I have to be honest I am not 100% sure. It looks like some pieces of medieval jewellery to me but you'll have a better idea."

He handed over four small clear, polythene envelopes which were stapled to the submission forms in each case, all of which contained 10-figure grid references identifying the place where they were found, almost to the exact blade of grass.

Dorothy took them carefully in her hand and after a quick look started repeating the word "wow" over and over again.

David took this as a good sign and decided it was probably a good time to find out where the silver coins had been found.

"Let me know what you think of them in due course," he said casually. "That was an interesting story about the William 1 ransom. Is there likely to be any truth in it?"

"Most likely," said Dorothy looking up from the little envelopes with reluctance. "The coins themselves were Silver Merks, as you may know, and the ransom was 10,000 marks after all. Merks were unusual and we haven't seen any more like this in my department so it is possible they were coined at Melrose specifically for the purpose of the ransom for William I. Unfortunately we may never know as the finder died two months ago. Tragic really, as they appeared to be in a classic hoard pattern, as if a plough or something was peeling them out of their hiding place one at a time."

"Whereabouts were they found?" chipped in Clive, unable to hide his boyish enthusiasm.

Dorothy looked at them and then at the envelopes in her hand. "I shouldn't really divulge such information but I know I can trust you both to use it wisely. They were found somewhere on High Ruston Farm. The person concerned was not up to speed with grid references etc. so I can't say any more accurately than that."

David looked at Clive who nodded briefly to indicate that he knew the farm. They made further knowledgeable small talk with Dorothy and retired to the Wagon soon afterwards to discuss the evening's revelations.

"What do you think?" asked Clive, deferring as usual to his more experienced companion.

"It's a really interesting prospect, isn't it? Imagine if there was a hoard of medieval money just lying about on High Ruston Farm. Dot seemed convinced it was quite likely, and she'll know if anyone does. It would be pretty cool actually looking for something specific for a change. Do you know the people at the farm?"

Clive nodded. "They seem fairly relaxed folk. I know them through the PTA. Hopefully they'll allow us to search the farm. I'll phone and sound them out. Sounds like they already agreed to let somebody detect on their land."

"We should draw up an agreement in case we do find something valuable. In fact we should both sign it ourselves so that we split anything 50/50. Agreed?"

Clive nodded and smiled.

"I'll draw up an agreement. There are some standard ones available on the internet. But you are agreed that whoever finds anything on High Ruston splits it with the other?"

"What if one of us is out on their own and finds something?" asked Clive.

"It doesn't matter. If either of us finds anything on High Ruston, we share it evenly. I have heard of plenty of people who have fallen out over this kind of thing. Agreed?"

"Yeh, of course," confirmed Clive, but without conviction. David noticed this and had the start of an uneasy feeling about his friend.

They talked for a while longer about the evening's presentation and recent finds until they judged it sensible to return home to their respective wives.

As they left the pub Clive confirmed that he would speak to the owners of the farm and clear it with them to detect on the land.

David sought reassurance one more time regarding the share of any finds.

"I'll draw up an agreement for us both to sign, just so that everything is above board. Okay?"

"Yeh, yeh of course," said Clive, clearly lost in thoughts of what might be buried in the soil of High Ruston Farm. He was also wondering if it would be possible, after he got permission to search, to get out alone before he would have to invite David along. If the farmers knew where the other coins had been found then he had a chance to find any hoard and keep it and any credit for himself.

They smiled and waved as they got into their cars, and all looked fine from a distance. Clive's face though, hid a strong and selfish desire to find the missing ransom money for William the Lion and to steal the credit for himself. Whatever the value of the hoard, it was nothing to the kudos it would bestow upon him amongst the detectorist fraternity. Not to mention the never-ending gratitude of Dr Dorothy Pitches and her team. He could see himself addressing learned audiences in Edinburgh and London as her guest. Most likely any London trip would require the two of them to stay overnight in the same hotel and who knows what might happen in such circumstances? Perhaps an honour might not be too much to hope for. His imagination ran wild with the possibilities of it all.

For his part David left that evening with the distinct suspicion that there had not been a complete meeting of their minds regarding the sharing of anything found. Added to that was the fact that he did not know the farmers at all while Clive did. Surely after all the help he had provided to Clive he could trust him to keep that agreement? Surely? But there had been something distant in Clive's voice as he agreed to it. A certain lack of attention in his gaze.

"Better get that agreement drawn up and signed pronto," he thought to himself as he drove home. "You can't be too careful when something as valuable as this is at stake."

Chapter 9

Distrust and the Missing Hoard

Ever since the gold sovereign incident there had been an element of distrust between them. Clive had been out detecting on his own and had found a handful of coins. When they spoke next, David was surprised to find his friend slightly evasive about the day's finds. Normally they would both detail what they had found including the dates and condition of any coins, no matter how commonplace. Instead Clive had simply referred to his finds that day as junk and then later as nothing interesting although he had mentioned finding some coins. Clive also cut the conversation short as if he didn't want to discuss the day's finds any further.

When David headed out detecting the next day he discovered that his own headphones weren't working. As usual he popped round to Clive's to borrow one of his sets and found that Clive was already out detecting again, although it hadn't been mentioned during the recent conversation. Clive's wife Ruth showed the way to his study and left David to help himself to whatever kit he needed. As far as she was concerned if David stole it all, sold it and Clive could never go or talk about metal detecting ever again that was fine by her. She knew David 's wife felt exactly the same way. Both had spent hours half listening to enthusiastic descriptions of finds, knowing they would never get those hours back.

The headphones were in a prominent place over the back of a chair but David decided to have a poke about amongst the other bits and pieces. In a clear plastic coin envelope, half hidden under Clive's mouse mat he noticed a familiar looking coin. It was a Victorian gold sovereign and had a small label on it with the previous days date on it and the name High Ruston Farm which they had never yet searched together.

David was annoyed. He had always been scrupulous about letting his friend know about all the exciting finds he had made, and here was evidence that Clive had been withholding one of the best finds either had had so far. It was the first ever piece of gold found by either of them. On top of that it was clear that Clive had already obtained clearance to search in the area of the missing ransom hoard without inviting David along. He grabbed the headphones in a temper and left. Later that night he got a phone call from his friend who started enthusing about a gold sovereign he had found the previous day. David listened and wondered if he would have heard the story without calling in to borrow the equipment earlier. Clive's claim of initially not realising what he had found was dubious to say the least. The sovereign was distinctive and very different from the run of the mill copper coins they found by the dozen or the occasional more exciting silver ones. To make matters worse there was still no mention of High Ruston Farm. David listened but said little, deciding that from that moment on all agreements were void, and it was every man for himself regarding William the Lion's missing silver.

Chapter 10

Robbie Buchanan

The phantom pains in Robbie's missing right leg had woken him up yet again. If only it was still attached he could scratch it or pinch it or even cut the bloody thing off; just something to stop the pain. But he couldn't because it wasn't there. It was somewhere in Qatar or Saudi, depending on where the actual operation had been performed to cut it off. He knew there had been no option. Two bullets had ripped it apart at the middle thigh and knee, one hitting an artery. It all happened in Iraq, where he had no legitimate reason to be at the time. In fact he had been part of a covert team extracting an undercover source from Amara before he became compromised. As it turned out it was slightly after he had been compromised and things had got messy. Robbie had gone in with a team of ex-special forces soldiers now working for MI6s paramilitary wing, enigmatically named 'The Increment'. Although he had never been a soldier he had gone through a pretty rigorous selection process and training and worked with these guys a lot. They provided the muscle to get in and out of anywhere and he had the detailed brief to select and finger the required target. Sometimes it was an assassination mission but mainly they extracted friendly assets from very unfriendly situations. It had been fun, usually. He had enjoyed the adrenalin rush of such jobs, especially compared to a desk job in Whitehall or GCHQ, which had been the fate of some of his fellow trainees. The troops he worked with always slagged him off as a civvy but he knew to the penny what each of them got paid for the work they did, and he would rather be on his pay rate than theirs. Either way, once things kicked off, it didn't matter how each man had got there and he knew he could handle whatever came his way.

He had been selected straight from university. Studying Russian and Arabic had marked him out as a candidate for intelligence work even before he had realised it, and after a brief membership of the university's Officer Training Corps, his progress was followed with interest by several government agencies. He had left the OTC by mutual agreement when he refused to get his hair cut short and focussed instead on his athletic interests. Robbie could have played most sports to a high standard but running was his strongest suit. He finished his final academic year with a bronze medal in the Commonwealth Games 800 metres whilst waiting to graduate with a double first in languages. As he was starting to prepare a CV and consider application forms or a gap year he was phoned out of the blue on his mobile by a civil servant who wanted to meet and offer him a job. The initial chat over coffee led to other meetings with other people until he found himself on a selection week with other young graduates and some criminals at a large house an hour or so outside London.

Robbie had excelled at every aspect of the selection process and at the end of the week was offered a place on an accelerated programme within what he had initially believed to be the Foreign Office (or was it the Home Office; he was hazy now as to which he had been working towards). Training continued, and it became clear from the number of military and rather shifty personnel involved that he was not part of any conventional Graduate Trainee programme. This became official during the last month or so of his training when he was taken aside and told that his security clearance was complete, something he was unaware was happening, and he was formally offered a post within MI6 at an eye-watering starting salary which he was informed included the X Factor for life-threatening service.

A young man in search of adventure, he had jumped at the chance and was initially posted to a liaison department in GCHQ. He graduated to carrying 'Diplomatic Bags' on a variety of flights all over the world

The Treasure Hunters

and was eventually seconded to The Increment, initially as an administrator. Administrator meant he did whatever he was asked by his line manager, a tough ex-military officer who seemed to have spent most of his life in either Africa or the Middle East. He carried out refresher training on weapons and started providing local support for missions. Then he was on missions. Then he was bleeding to death in a taxi in Damascus with the extracted agent pressing the main artery in his thigh to slow the bleeding with little prospect of saving Robbie's life. This was clear from the fact that the agent was simultaneously talking on his mobile phone, effectively taking over Robbie's mission. Just as well really, as Robbie blacked out in the taxi and woke up three weeks later in the British military hospital in Cyprus.

He later pieced together what had happened while he "slept on the job" as his boss put it. He and the asset had got separated from the main group while Robbie collected him from the safe house. He had judged that going there mob-handed would have drawn attention to their target. As it turned out their opposite numbers had figured out who was the leak at their end and arrived at the safe house just as Robbie was leaving. He had shot one local agent and managed to escape from the other two down a fire escape with his asset, but not before stopping two bullets in the leg. The two men had stopped a taxi at gun point, leaving the other MI6 members to shoot it out with the locals. They had narrowly escaped in the opposite direction leaving one of the opposition dead and two with minor gunshot wounds. Robbie blanked out and the rescued agent called in for back-up. British back-up was thin on the ground but it had officially been a joint British/US intelligence operation and the Americans sent in enough helicopters to liberate Texas. As a result Robbie made it to a US carrier just in time to save his life if not his right leg. It had been removed somewhere along the route to Cyprus from where he eventually was flown back to Blighty.

Death, injuries and amputations aside, Robbie found that the mission had been judged a success and there were tea and medals for all involved, especially those above him in the food chain. For his part, he knew as soon as he regained consciousness that his active career was over. There was little chance of trying for the Gold Medal in the next Commonwealth Games either. He had little appetite for the Paralympics or the working equivalent, which was a desk job in London. After protracted negotiations due to his age, he was offered pay for life at a lower grade if he disappeared and kept quiet about everything he knew, including how he had lost his leg.

It was therefore a bit of a surprise when he received a phone call from Jennifer Allerdyce at MI6 asking him to do a little job for her. The first surprising thing was that the call came through on a pay-as-you-go mobile phone which he only used for personal calls. The second was that MI6 believed he still gave a shit about them. The final surprising thing was that they believed he could still be of use to Queen and country. It was this final aspect which intrigued him enough to keep listening rather than to throw the phone into the river where he was fishing and immediately buy a replacement.

"I would like you to do a little bit of detective work for me in a village in the Scottish Borders called Kirkton. Have you ever heard of it?" asked Jennifer.

"No," replied Robbie in all honesty before adding, "but then I haven't heard of Jennifer Allerdyce either. You know that I am retired from MI6 on medical grounds don't you?"

"According to your file, which I currently hold in my hand, you are not in fact retired but are still on our books as an employee. I notice also that you have not actually carried out any work for us for almost four years. On the face of it I think you owe us a little bit of work, Mr Buchanan. I can assure you that this particular job will be far safer than your previous assignments and we will, of course, cover all expenses. All you have to do is stay in Kirkton for as long as it takes to discover who found five million dollars or so of currency belonging to our American cousins, which unfortunately fell out of a helicopter during a storm. We are certain that somebody very local to the area found it. Your cover story is that you are writing a book about rare native flora and fauna in the Scottish Borders as part of a European-funded effort to reverse their decline. This should give you scope to roam about with a camera and speak to locals who might have been wandering about the area when the cash went missing."

"In case the file missed it out, I am limited these days in terms of roaming over the countryside. What if I say no?"

"Well Mr Buchanan, Robbie if I may call you that, times are hard here in Whitehall and it is quite difficult to justify the cost of staff at the best of times, even some of the most hardworking ones. I would find it extremely difficult to defend the payment of a full salary to somebody who does not actually carry out any work for the department at all. Before you make any protest about agreements with any of my predecessors here let me just inform you that none of the circle of staff who agreed that cosy little deal with you when you left are still working here. In other words, Robbie, all deals are up for renegotiation if I so choose.

"But let's not start on the wrong foot, no pun intended. If you carry out this little job for me, then everything can continue as before. You can continue to hide in Kingussie, wherever that may be, and collect a salary for sitting about doing nothing. Find whoever became-rich-quick in Kirkton and I will not only be forever grateful but I will personally sign off your previous arrangement, meaning as long as I serve, you are safe. What do you say?"

Robbie was about to tell her exactly where to go when he thought better of it. It could be a bluff on her part but he was not entirely sure. A lot of grey areas had been investigated to allow him to leave with a salary rather than a disability pension and that had all been agreed in the glow of what had been seen as the successful outcome of a particularly sensitive mission. If it was true that none of the original signatories to the deal were still there, then this Jennifer woman could actually put a spanner in the works. On the other hand, how tough would it be to spend some time in a sleepy little Borders village and spot the local with money to burn?

"Okay Jennifer, I'll pop down there and have a look, on the condition that you confirm my position with the company whether I find the cash or not."

"I am pleased to hear you will try but I will find it easier to justify your current circumstances if you are

65

successful. I can say no more than that. You are booked into the Wagon Hotel from tomorrow onwards for seven nights. If that proves insufficient time then find some cheaper accommodation thereafter. Good luck."

"How will I get in touch with you?" asked Robbie.

"You won't need to. I'll keep in touch with you. As the editor of Rare Species Monthly I feel that is the least I can do."

Before Robbie could say another word the line went dead. He was hacked off, it was true, and to prove it he threw the mobile into the river. If she was that interested in him she would soon track down the next one he bought. Let her earn her money too, he thought.

The next day Robbie Googled Kirkton on his laptop, packed enough clothes for a week and threw everything into his car. He was annoyed at being tracked down and called out of retirement. He was more annoyed at having so little in his day-to-day life that he could actually jump in a car and drive away at such short notice, without anybody being inconvenienced. He also had to admit to himself that there was a part of him that wanted to rise to the challenge and find out what had happened to MI6's money, or the CIA's money, or whoever had owned it at the time of its loss.

He hadn't had to work since he left MI6 and as a result hadn't actually done much. Beyond medical appointments and fittings for new prosthetic legs, he had read a huge amount, tried out several hobbies which all failed to grab his attention and decided not to drink himself to death. His old athlete's habits had helped there and he ate well and exercised regularly as best he could now. He swam regularly and could now walk on level ground at around the same pace as he had with two legs. He had travelled a lot at first, principally around the British Isles and Scotland in particular, finally settling in Kingussie. Beyond that though, he had not really taken on any fresh challenge the way he had once been driven to do.

This little task from Ms Allerdyce had awoken the old competitive instincts again.

"You have a week." "Then I'll solve it in three days."

He found himself enjoying the drive South to Kirkton. It was, after all, the first time he had travelled anywhere with a purpose for some considerable time. As he drove he began to think through how best to go about the task. He knew that the money had been jettisoned one mile from Kirkton in the proximity of an electricity pylon. The helicopter had struggled on for a further five miles, clearing a range of hills before finally crashing on the edge of a military training area. The containers which had been used to carry the cash and which were fitted with tracking devices had been found eight hours later near Scotch Corner in the back of a cattle truck with a driver who had been checked out and monitored ever since. It seemed likely that the driver had no knowledge of the previous contents of the containers. The village, or villages, and surrounding area had a population around four hundred people of all ages. The crash had occurred close to the village, outwith the shooting, fishing or tourist seasons. It was therefore most likely that a local person had found the cash, switched it from the original containers and created a false trail by throwing them onto a truck which they knew or suspected would be travelling away from the village very soon.

The task therefore boiled down to creating a list of everyone in the villages who was there at the time, was physically able to do all that and could not be ruled out for any other reason. "Simples," he thought. A list of four hundred people to start with was big but from the information Jennifer had already sent him over half could be ruled out straight away by virtue of age and health or being away at the time. Further checks were under way to rule people out, including a rather obscure one to identify anyone in the area who had won half a million pounds or more in National Lottery. It had been surprising how many people were recorded as being on holiday abroad via their passport usage. It must be a well-travelled and affluent village, thought Robbie.

He had been given a contact in London who would be able to check out any leads he had and to confirm anyone who could be ruled out. This contact would have access to bank accounts etc, although Robbie guessed nobody would be foolish enough to deposit the money into their high street bank or building society account. He had to get to know people, get them talking and find out the most likely locals to be wandering about close to midnight in the rain near an electricity pylon.

His mood was rising at the prospect of the challenge the nearer he got to Kirkton and he was finding it harder and harder to hate Jennifer Allerdyce completely for picking on him. He could hate her a bit for the way she had spoken to him and threatened him but he was actually quite grateful to feel useful again.

By the time he had arrived at Kirkton his contact had called to say a list had been emailed with 117 names on it. It was hoped that this could be trimmed back further when all the mobile phone records were in and people's whereabouts could be confirmed from them. Unfortunately one of the networks had a dodgy transmitter in the area and had decided it wasn't worth the effort to replace it for such a low number of customers. As a result the whereabouts of their customers could not be verified unless they had been elsewhere that night.

Robbie decided that 117 sounded a lot better than four hundred. If that number could be cut further by the next day so much the better. For now he had to focus on a low key arrival at the Wagon Hotel and look convincingly like someone who gave a monkey's about the areas wildlife.

He drove into the main street and saw an elderly gentleman sitting on the wall of the first house on the left. The man was sitting on a small cushion, suggesting that he often perched there and watched the world go by. Robbie decided that he might as well get started straight away and stopped to ask directions.

"Can you tell me the way to the Wagon Hotel please?" he asked politely, trying to use the question to start a conversation.

The man looked at him without any expression and replied, "Can do, if that SatNav of yours can't."

Robbie wasn't ready for that but recovered quickly to lie: "It's playing up a bit."

"Aye, they do, I gather," said the old man in a friendlier tone. "Keep going along the main street here and it's on the right there. There's a big sign sticking out and there'll be a blue Vectra badly parked outside by now."

"Thanks," said Robbie with a smile. "You live here then?"

"Aye," said the old man, with a look suggesting their first conversation was at an end.

He's probably done a resistance to interrogation course, thought Robbie, and drove off hoping the directions from the SatNav weren't loud enough for the man to hear.

The Wagon Hotel was an old coaching house whose fortunes had risen or declined dependent on the fortunes of successive owners over the years. The general appearance of the place suggested lean times at present. As the elderly gentleman had predicted, there was a blue Vectra badly parked outside. Robbie noticed amongst the day to day scrapes and dents there was a large V shape divot in the rear bumper which neatly corresponded to the pattern of a lamppost opposite the pub.

Robbie got himself into character. He was here to discover which of the rare species which had been recorded in the area in the past, were still prevalent today. The best way to do this was to ask all the locals which species they saw on a regular basis, especially while out walking in the surrounding area. This, it was felt, gave him a good reason to be asking who might have been out and about in the area where the money was lost (and found) on the appropriate night. Robbie's knowledge of endangered native species was sparse to say the least, but a selection of links had been sent to his email address via his point of contact at MI6 and he was destined for an intensive course of studies in his hotel room on the first night.

Despite the rather down-at-heel exterior of the hotel, Robbie found a young and pretty girl behind the counter in the public bar who was expecting him, had taken the time to remember his name from their booking records and made him feel very welcome. She had even paid attention to the note in the booking that he was 'ambulent disabled'. As a result she offered to help with his modest luggage and stressed they had re-arranged bookings so that he would be on the ground floor, close to both the bar and the dining room. She asked if he would be dining in the hotel that evening and what time he would like breakfast the next morning? Also, if that would be the same time each morning? Such was the genuine interest and professionalism that he started to look forward to his stay. The fact that she was very pretty, had a trim figure and kept smiling at him helped too.

It wasn't till sometime much later that he realised with regret that she had not reappeared after that first night, during his stay at the Wagon. Perhaps she had gone on holiday or maybe had been sacked for being so professional and normal and thus showing up the rest of the staff and the owners.

Having been given the password for the WiFi, Robbie logged in and found a number of emails from his point of contact. The number of 'possibles' was down to 64, although it was emphasised that he had to try to sweep up any recent arrivals or temporary residents who might have to be considered. A message with 27 links to articles on rare species in the Scottish Borders suggested somebody had been busy researching on his behalf. He sat down on the bed and removed his prosthetic leg which had been rubbing at the stump of his thigh during the journey. Then he lay down, convincing himself that he would not dose off if he did. In a few minutes, however, he was sound asleep.

He woke up just before the official end of service for food in the pub and, finding himself starving, rushed down to catch an evening meal. The young lady who had shown him in earlier was now behind the bar and re-assured him that he was still in time for hot food. The bar had around twelve people in it by then including a middle aged lady with bright dyed red hair, who was sitting intimately in a corner table with a man of similar age. Declining the offer of a table in the separate dining room, Robbie nodded hello to the other faces and ordered a pint of real ale while he waited for his fisherman's pie.

"You're an inmate then," said a middle aged man in a friendly manner.

"Yes," replied Robbie. "Seems a nice enough place."

He said it in a way which left it open for the man to agree or disagree as he wished.

"Aye, it's a friendly enough place and the food's good now Kev's in the kitchen. The fisherman's pie is one of his specialities. You here for work or pleasure then?" the man asked in friendly rather than nosey way.

"Bit of each really," said Robbie. "I'm carrying out some research on the rarer species in the area for a specialist publication. I need to get a handle on any of the wildlife which is getting more scarce in the valley."

There was a bit of a pause suggesting that nobody found this task interesting in any way shape or form but another of the locals who turned out to be called George chipped in.

"You never see adders anymore."

Robbie waited for a follow up comment but there was none.

"Were they more common in the past?" Robbie ventured, hoping it was nobody's specialist subject until he had time to read up on them properly.

"Oh yes, you couldn't move for them at one time. Then they made them protected and you never see a trace now."

A powerful looking man of forty or so in a set of John Deere overalls joined the conversation

"I saw one a month or so back. They are still about, but not as many as when I was a schoolboy. Then you had to watch out."

"What do you think caused their numbers to dwindle then?" asked Robbie, glad to be in a conversation with so many villagers so early on in his stay.

"Jack shot them all," added a man in a suit, indicating the farmer in the John Deere kit.

"Rubbish. A few maybe, but only a few."

"This guy will have you in hand-cuffs for it," continued the man in the suit pointing at Robbie.

"I'm only researching the reasons, not locking up the culprits. Anyway it's not restricted to adders. Anything which people would have seen on a regular basis years ago, which has now all but disappeared. There has been a similar study on the other side of the border," Robbie embellished before realising he may have made a mistake.

"Whereabouts?" asked the man in the suit who seemed pretty sharp.

"I'm not sure exactly," Robbie said. "I wasn't involved in it at all."

"The animals all left that side of the border cause the beer's pish," said the man in the suit and the others laughed.

"The big cat has eaten a lot of the local wildlife," said George.

"Oh no, here we go," said Jack.

"Oh yes it has. I've seen it loads of times," continued George. "Not a tiger obviously but something big with huge black ears."

"Mickey Mouse," chipped in Andy in the suit.

"Not a mouse, something much bigger. A big cat. A lynx or something. Must have been a pet and it's got loose."

"Who the fuck had a pet tiger in Kirkton?" asked Andy in mock exasperation.

"Not a tiger, a lynx," persisted George. "It's eaten all the wildlife for miles."

Robbie was relieved when his dinner arrived and he could excuse himself with feigned reluctance from the argument at the bar. He sat at a table opposite the group and watched as they gently kidded George about 'the beast of the Rowent valley'.

It was clearly a regular theme and the banter was in relative friendly tones. Robbie pretended to focus on his fisherman's pie while the crowd at the bar moved from big cats to local gossip. Some of them left, presumably for their own homes while others arrived. Slowly but a surely a large group started to form at a corner table. They stood out from the crowd at the bar as they all had clipboards or notebooks and most ordered soft drinks. It was clearly a business meeting or at least a business-like meeting that they were here for. The group centred around a man in his early sixties who seemed to be the chairman. He had a quiet word with each member as they arrived after a friendly hello. It looked like he was gathering support for something and checking how many votes he had in the bag.

George from the bar shouted over at the chairman. "Robbie here is looking for snakes, Henry."

Henry smiled the smile of someone who had heard it all before, much of it from George and continued his discussion with the latest of his group to arrive.

"Not just snakes, mind. Big cats too."

Henry smiled again and looked over at Robbie to assess the merits of George's information. He saw Robbie looking fairly embarrassed and when they made eye contact Robbie explained quickly that he was researching all species of wildlife which were in decline in the area although he didn't expect to see any big cats.

"Oh yes, big bastard with black pointy ears," added George to nobody in particular.

Henry Parker walked over to Robbie and introduced himself as the chairman of the local community council and asked if there was anything that the council could perhaps do to help? Henry was sure the members would rally round such a valuable activity.

Robbie saw a chance and leapt at it.

"I am trying to identify species which were commonly seen in the area and which have gone into decline. At this point I am looking for anecdotal stuff, who saw what, where and when. The results will lead to further studies into specific species and look at ways to reverse the trends. If I could get information from all the members of the council or village, that would be really useful."

Henry nodded his head indicating to all who knew him that it would be easy enough and he would organise it.

"The next meeting is tomorrow night in the village hall. Come along and say a few words there if you like."

"I thought that was the meeting tonight," said Robbie.

"No, I thought we'd better meet beforehand, as the proposed extension to the caravan park is up for discussion again. You're lucky, it'll be a full house. I'll let you speak early so you can slip away before the toys get thrown out of the cots and the handbags start swinging."

"Great," said Robbie thinking the meeting might be quite fun by the sound of it.

"Meeting starts at seven sharp. God knows when it will finish tomorrow though. I'm taking sandwiches."

Henry shook Robbie's hand and returned to his table where he clearly briefed his team on Robbie and his mission.

Ideal, Robbie thought to himself. With a bit of luck the whole village will be there and I can start to put faces to these names. It wouldn't do any harm to hear them speak either. You never know. Someone might just let something slip.

Robbie picked up his plate and cutlery and carried it to the bar to save the overworked girl a trip. He also fancied another pint of that real ale. A few new faces had arrived since he had sat down and maybe he could have a chat with some of them. Apart from anything else he was starting to enjoy having company for a change. He had spent too long on his own since he had left MI6.

"The fisherman's pie was delicious," he said. "Another pint of Border Treasure please."

"Is Henry going to help you track down the big cat then?" asked George.

"A fat cat maybe," replied Robbie. "By the way, what are you drinking?"

Chapter 11

George

George Rawlings had been born just outside Kirkton in a large farmhouse which his travelling salesman father had rented for years. He had attended school in neighbouring Kelso rather than Kirkton itself for reasons known only to his mother. As a result he was something of an enigma amongst the Kirkton born and bred of his era. They had known him from school holidays and from occasional visits to Sunday school but not as a true contempory. This effect was enhanced by the fact that his parents were from Newcastle, his father was away from home a lot and George himself had moved to Northumberland to work when he was in his very early twenties. He had of course returned to the village when he retired in his fifties, some twenty or so years ago. He was therefore from Kirkton but not of it in the eyes of many of the true locals.

His working life had been a rich mixture of success and failure, first as an apprentice in the offices of a shipbuilders then a succession of his own ventures followed by a lucrative final stint as a salesman for the business which had employed his father. It had been this final twenty year stretch which had provided a fairly generous pension which allowed him to survive thereafter and pursue his hobbies of fishing, golf and confusing visitors to the village pubs.

In his younger days he had been a scratch golfer, famed throughout the area as a sportsman, bon-viveur and ladies' man. He had fished all his life, on rivers, from beaches and at sea. In Kirkton, only Callum the Ghillie knew more about salmon fishing than George and that was in doubt amongst some.

He had married a society heiress against her family's wishes and to his own surprise. They had had two children and almost ten years together of apparent bliss. George continued his job as a travelling sales rep, feeling that it was his duty to bring in a wage whether they needed it or not. As a result, he was away a lot of the time and his wife grew as bored as he grew lonely on the road alone. In retrospect it was only a question of which one of them would weaken first. As his friends had predicted it was George, who accepted more than just the usual hospitality of a Glasgow landlady one evening. Thereafter the clock was ticking on the bomb that was their marriage.

When George confessed to his wife one night, racked with genuine guilt, she flew into a rage and their marriage was over. George's circle of fashionable and wealthy friends closed round the injured party which was his wife, a circle which included her two boyfriends. George found himself ostracised at the golf club, in the neighbourhood where he had lived and was told in no uncertain terms that he should not darken the doorstep of his in-laws ever again. He moved to a small flat in North Shields till the divorce was settled. His wife's solicitor visited him with disdain and talked through the need for a quick solution to his philandering, as he put it, for the sake of the children. Still feeling guilty, he had accepted the offer of £20,000 to finalise the matter of the matrimonial home. Had he been thinking straight and hired his own lawyer he could have held out for a million or so.

Soon afterwards when his wife remarried an old flame the pennies started to drop. By then he had lost his kids, his home and a luxurious lifestyle. He took the offer of early retirement and travelled round Europe for two years decidedly off the rails. A combination of drink and drugs took its toll on his faculties, while women of easy commercial virtue separated him from both his marital settlement and his redundancy payment quite quickly. By the end of the Grand Tour he was no longer the man he had once been. He was broke aside from his pension, emotionally broken and mentally suffering from drink and drug abuse on a huge scale. His only chance of happiness lay with a return to his earliest memories and Kirkton. He managed to secure a small house to rent and there struggled to come to terms with loneliness, reduced circumstances and significant brain damage.

The good people of Kirkton tried to help George where they could, but both parties found it difficult to connect and as a result he became a welcome enough but somewhat remote figure in the village. From the village but not of it, as ever.

Chapter 12

Village Life

All life was here in Kirkton. After only a few days in the village Robbie had become privy to a wealth of stories about local inhabitants both living and dead. Had the script writers of a soap opera struggled for inspiration, a week in Kirkton would have provided a wealth of fresh material. The permutations of who was living or sleeping with whom and who had previously been living or sleeping with who else seemed endless according to some people's accounts. Robbie was glad, however, for the piece of advice Jennifer had given him about arriving in a small village: "Always assume you are talking to someone related to whoever you are talking about and you won't go far wrong."

This had so far saved his embarrassment at least twice. He might have added to her advice to assume whoever you are talking to has been sleeping with whoever you are talking about. This held true with a number of his new found friends at The Wagon Hotel. At least two ladies of quite different age groups had definitely shown more than a passing interest in the village's latest visitor and in the case of the thirty something barmaid at The Wagon, who served him on his second night, he had no strong desire to resist.

Donna the barmaid had seemed initially a likely source of intelligence on the regulars and many of the two villages' other inhabitants. It soon transpired that she would much rather talk about herself and how unhappy she was with her tractor driver husband. No matter how often Robbie managed to steer a conversation on to one of the locals on his list, Donna would always manage to steer it back to herself and how tough her life was. Robbie would have given up listening very quickly if she had not had large full breasts which permanently strained for freedom from her collection of low cut tops. At first he had resisted the temptation to stare at them when she propped them on the bar right in front of his face as they spoke. When he paid no apparent attention to her cleavage she seemed to lean forward revealing more flesh. This would continue by degrees until Robbie was left unsure whether it would be ruder to stare or not to stare at her breasts. In the end, instinct always won out and he would find himself staring at her beautiful bust. At this point she would feign shock and walk away to some invented task always to return in due course to continue their previous conversation.

He had written out a list of all the locals he could already identify from his London source and annotated on the list who would have been likely to be out and about at night on the date the money went missing. His plan was then to delete anyone he could say was absent or unable to have seen and collected the cash for definite as he got to know their circumstances in detail. Whoever it was would have had to find the money and transfer it from the original containers in the eight hours between the helicopter hitting the pylons outside Kirkton and Robbie Roberton waking up and beginning his journey to Barton Services. That meant the guilty party would most likely be able bodied, have a reason to be outdoors at night and be smart enough to realise the containers were fitted with tracking devices. He reasoned that it couldn't be that difficult to narrow down the suspects to a small enough number to pass on to Jennifer. Thereafter she could check out each one and see who might have come into a large amount of money without a reasonable explanation. There couldn't be that many people out and about at night here he reckoned. But then he reckoned without the inhabitants of Kirkton and their many and varied nocturnal activities.

From Donna, Robbie learned little of use about the locals on his list. He did learn a lot about Donna and how long were the hours of the average tractor driver's day.

Most of all though, he learned that he himself was lonely, very lonely indeed.

Chapter 13

The Community Council Meeting

The night following Robbie's arrival, he made his way to the village hall in plenty of time for the meeting. He had spent the day studying wildlife and making up a questionnaire to distribute which he hoped would harvest a lot of information about the habits of the villagers. It was unlikely that anyone would write "I last saw an adder the night I pocketed about $6 million or so in cash" but perhaps by deduction he could rule some people in or out from their written returns.

As he approached the Village Hall he realised that Henry Parker had not exaggerated the interest in the Caravan Site extension issue. A number of large groups were in deep conversation outside the hall and cars were parked all along the main street, many of them well-used farmers' pickups. The door of the hall was wide open and people were heading inside all the time.

When he arrived at the door and said "Hello" to a group of locals nearby they stared at him with suspicion. He ignored them and went inside. There he found that the hall was already fit to bursting point and there were no free seats. He was about to head back outside when Henry took him by the arm and directed him towards the stage.

"It's worse than I thought," he confided in Robbie. "At least two people have brought their solicitors with them. They seem to forget that the planning application decision rests entirely with the local authority. As a community council we can submit views but they have no statutory requirement to pay any attention. I suppose people just want to let off steam as usual and the Community Council, as ever, is the most convenient point of impact. I'll cover the basics and introduce you. Don't feel obliged to stay after you have spoken. It could turn nasty as the night goes on."

"I wouldn't miss it for the world," thought Robbie as he made his way to the stage.

At exactly seven o'clock by Henry's expensive-looking watch, he called the meeting to order. It actually took a further ten minutes before everyone squeezed inside the hall and the conversations stopped.

"I would like to welcome everyone to tonight's meeting of the Kirkton Community Council. The agenda for tonight has been posted in the shop and on the website but there are copies on some of the seats for those who missed it."

"What about the bloody caravan site?" shouted someone from the back of the hall. "That's what we are all here for. Get on with it!"

"I think you will find that in the agenda as item five," countered Henry unfazed and clearly ready for a lively evening. "We will stick to the agenda as there are a number of important issues to discuss tonight besides the caravan site."

"Like what?" came the question from the same voice as before.

"I'm glad you asked that," replied Henry, as ever unmoved by the emotions of the crowd. "Item two concerns us all. Mr Buchanan here is carrying out a survey of endangered species in the area and I am hopeful that we can all help him with his task."

Robbie stood up very briefly so that the assembled mass could recognise him and to confirm that he had nothing whatsoever to do with the Caravan Site extension. There was a very brief round of applause from somewhere in the hall before Henry continued.

"We also have item six which relates to the need for new members of the council, which I am pleased will be aired with so many of the village present."

The basic matters of the minutes were covered along with the first item which related to a rubber stamping of funds for the Primary School's garden project. There was some heckling along the way but Henry appeared to combine the patience of a saint, the energy of a modern Hercules with the thick skin of a rhino. As a result after only twenty minutes or so, Robbie found that he was called upon to speak.

"I would like to thank the chairman for this opportunity to address many of the village. I am here as part of a preliminary study of declining species of flora and fauna within the Rowent Valley."

He proceeded with the confidence which his briefing notes and references had provided and introduced the questionnaire. As he held up the bundle of freshly printed sheets he was relieved to find that several people appeared from the stage and elsewhere and distributed them to the gathered mass on his behalf.

"There are boxes for the return of the sheets in the Village Shop, the Wagon, the post office and the Reiver," added Henry most helpfully. "The sooner they are returned the sooner Mr Buchanan can begin his work."

Robbie smiled and felt things were going well considering he had only been in the village for two days.

"Are there any questions?" he asked.

One of the members of the community council put her hand up and stood up when Henry pointed to her.

"Should we hold a raffle to raise funds for your project?" she asked.

Robbie was flattered at the level of support he was getting but confirmed that his work was already fully funded. "European money," he added.

"Bloody French," shouted a sheep farmer from the back of the hall.

Another hand went up in the middle of the hall. When Henry indicated that the figure had the floor a man of around seventy stood up and the assembly groaned.

"Do you think that an unnecessary extension of the existing Caravan Site will destroy even more of the natural habitat of our wildlife, causing even more work for you and your mates?" inquired the man unperturbed by his reception.

There were cheers and boos in equal measure from around the hall before Henry got to his feet and eventually restored order.

"Let's focus on one issue at a time, shall we? If there are no further questions for Mr Buchanan I would like to thank him for his interest in our wildlife and encourage everyone to fill in the questionnaire as thoroughly and timeously as possible."

There was a polite round of applause from the hall and Robbie sat down. While he waited for the applause to subside, Henry indicated to Robbie that he could leave if he so wished. Robbie indicated back that he was happy to stay, and a shrug of Henry's shoulders seemed to say, "you had your chance, mate".

From his seat on the stage Robbie could clearly see the audience below. With a bit of luck he could pick out some of the people on his list. It was a large list, he had to admit, but he had memorised as many of the possibles as he could. Now he could sit back and watch the fun with a bird's eye view. As he looked round the assembled faces he noticed the mass of dyed red hair and also noticed the lady underneath it was there with a different man from the one he had seen her with on the previous evening.

Items three and four concerned the fee for hiring a horse and the construction of a shed respectively. Robbie was not alone in finding both items relatively uninteresting, although a few people objected to the council paying for the village principal to ride a horse in

Edinburgh. Robbie was a bit confused as to why it was either necessary or contentious but watched the discussions with interest. His task in the village was greatly aided by Henry's suggestion that everyone who spoke introduce themselves first, a simple matter of name and street or house name.

After a vote of the members it was agreed that the horse would be fully funded and that the minutes would record that some villagers felt the new shed in Mr and Mrs Crawley's back garden was too large and should be painted to blend in with the neighbouring buildings, unlike their garage. Robbie caught the name Crawley and made sure he had a good look at the couple concerned.

There was a palpable rise in the tension in the hall as Henry announced item five, 'The Proposed Extension to The Caravan Park' through the acquisition of two acres of neighbouring farmland. To try to calm things down, Henry emphasised that the community council had no statutory powers to either approve or decline planning applications; that was a matter for the local authority, represented tonight by Mr Bob Ferguson the local councillor. Tonight's meeting would allow any local residents with views either way to air them in front of their councillor, who could then relay those views to the planning committee. Anyone who had strong objections to the proposal should submit them in written form to the council before the appropriate submission date. Henry then called on Bob Ferguson to outline the grounds for objection which would be considered by the committee and, in general terms, those that would not.

Robbie vaguely followed what was said but was far more interested in the villagers gathered in front of him. After Bob appealed for calm and hoped people would discuss things in a friendly and constructive way, Henry asked for questions from the floor.

A babble of questions and comments arose and he had to appeal for calm several times. He was assisted in this effort by a large uniformed police sergeant who chose this moment to stand up and stretch. Calm was thus restored and Henry pointed to the first hand he saw go up.

The hand belonged to the owner of the Wagon, who didn't live in the village and wasn't on Robbie's list. He spoke well and made valid points regarding the extra business which would be generated from more visitors to Kirkton, thus not only safeguarding existing jobs but creating additional employment in the area.

"Bloody typical," shouted a voice near the back for no apparent reason and the babble arose again.

Henry again managed to restore calm and indicated another hand, nearer the front.

"Bill Kent, retired teacher, Little Kirkton," the man attached to the hand announced.

Again there were groans which he ignored.

"The proposed extension will spoil the beautiful area of fields between the two villages and could lead to houses being built there too. It will ruin the view from my house and many others."

Bob Ferguson introduced a point of information that the effect on an individual's view was not valid grounds for objecting to a development.

"It bloody well should be," shouted Bill Kent who then sat down angrily.

The evening continued in a similar vein, with Henry heroically struggling to allow everyone a say, whether it was relevant or not. Robbie noticed the introductions grew longer as each speaker rose. Some whom he judged to be locals gave no introduction but the newer arrivals in the village felt the need to provide some background information. Most were comfortably retired from important positions where they had been respected automatically for their achievements. Here these achievements were unknown to most and the accompanying respect was therefore not forthcoming. As a result they felt the need to inform all present of their past achievements, often in great detail. How many staff they had been responsible for, the budget they had, world travel; the list went on and on. In each case it made no difference to the weight their opinion carried but it didn't stop them trying. In some cases the introductions were much longer than the questions and opinions of the council combined, and in one case the person was so engrossed in recalling his own career in shipping that by the end of his introduction he had forgotten the question he had planned to ask. Perhaps there had never been a question. There certainly seemed no obvious connection between shipping and caravans.

Robbie half-listened to the questions and discussions but paid close interest to the names of the speakers. By the end of the evening he had identified twelve of the people on his list and seen no obvious clues as to who may have found the money, beyond the Crawleys' overly large shed. He judged the event to have been very useful for his purposes, which was in stark contrast to the attendees who mainly felt it had been a waste of time.

Robbie was further surprised to be handed a total of eight completed questionnaires as people left, and the business card of a retired botanist from London, who offered any help he could provide.

Chapter 14

Barry The Gamekeeper

Barry Appleby had been raised on a farm in North Yorkshire where he had learned to shoot and to fish. Whilst he enjoyed fishing, he loved shooting; everything from clay pigeons to deer and anything in between. Rabbits, pheasants and partridges had little chance of escaping his aim from the age of seven or so upwards. He particularly liked to stock deer in the woods of the farm or the surrounding estates. By the time he left school, which as soon as he legally could, he was adept at thinning the population of any animals which were causing a nuisance on the farm. His skills were such that he was called in by all the neighbouring farmers from time to time and by the Forestry Commission when the deer population expanded to the point where cars were finding it difficult to miss them on the local roads. He won trophies for skeet and trap shooting and could double his wages from working on his father's farm just from selling the game he shot to local butchers and the rabbits to a pet food factory in Leeds.

His father had instilled in him a distrust of banks, paperwork and tax-returns in equal measure and as a result he preferred to deal in cash whenever he could. As a young boy he put his pocket money into a piggy bank bought for him by his father for the purpose. As he and his bundles of cash grew he progressed on to a safe in the wall of his bedroom by age fifteen, to one concreted into the floor of his room by age 21. The money piled up, even though he invested in new and better shotguns and a variety of all-terrain vehicles. He had learned to drive on the farm as soon as his feet could reach the pedals, and like many farmers' sons passed his driver test almost as soon as he turned 17.

He was however, very much his father's son and with a streak of stubbornness running through him a mile wide resisted his father's attempts to groom him to take over the farm. Things came to a head one evening in an inconclusive fist-fight between the two after the Friday auction had finished and they had retired to the local pub. Later that night Barry had packed his guns and the contents of his floor-safe into his pick-up and taken off to see the world. He had headed north for no reason other than his father's dislike of all things Scottish and had made it as far as Kirkton. There in the bar he had set eyes on Donna's mother, Judy, who was barmaid at The Reiver at the time and was as voluptuous as her daughter would later become. Barry had shoved a large bundle of notes into his pocket as he packed to leave home and when Judy saw the size of it she was smitten.

There followed a tempestuous affair between the two which lasted several years and became the talk of the valley. Judy had left her husband and moved into the farm cottage on a farm where Barry had secured work as a gamekeeper. Miraculously he had managed to buy the farm itself after two years and they had moved into the large farmhouse. Theirs seemed to be the romance of dreams until Judy got bored with Barry's long hours of work and deer stalking and took off one day with a tractor salesman from Taunton.

Barry was inconsolable and never recovered from the hurt and the shame of it all. Thereafter he kept himself to himself with only occasional visits to the Kirkton pubs. On these occasions he would say little and engage only in brief conversations about weather, fishing or shooting. His huge frame dissuaded anyone from mentioning Judy or even her daughter, who started work at The Wagon soon after. He was a solitary figure who seemed to dwell in a world of barely concealed hatred and anger. His six foot four figure was left well alone after Judy left and local people noted the marked reduction of the deer and rabbit population in the valley thereafter.

His pent-up anger was clearly visible, to those who were interested, in a number of traits in his behaviour. The drumming fingers on any flat surface, a knee which bounced up and down on the floor or barstool and his habit of straightening anything in his view, be it a picture, chair or row of beer mats. The other outlet for his inner, emotional turmoil was an unnaturally protective interest in Judy's daughter Donna, much to her discomfort. Barry would often appear towards the end of her shifts and frighten off any men showing too much interest in her or her cleavage. Few young men, locals or visitors, could withstand Barry's intimidating presence. The very few who could manage to weather that, often found themselves told to "Fuck off," when all else failed.

Donna's potential social life, outwith her marriage, was ruined by this approach on many an occasion. As she would moan to anyone who listened at the bar, Barry was not in any way related to her. Although he had lived with her mother for six years, he had never acted as a father then nor did her mother Judy ever include him in decisions about her future. This paternal interest had started after Judy ran off and many attributed it to an unhealthy interest in Donna herself. Either way, Barry slowly but surely scared off any local boy or man who might otherwise be tempted to have an affair with Donna. She was thus reduced to soliciting sympathy and comfort from visitors to the village and residents of the Hotel.

This gave many the feeling of being made supremely welcome while others got confused by the mixed signals emanating from the staff-side of the bar. This could be greatly increased by Barry's arrival late in the evening. Donna would be livid on such occasions and had even had a few blazing rows with Barry in full view of the clientele. A chink of light appeared when the owners bought a local house and needed the staff to take it in turns to stay overnight in the staff flat of the Reiver for legal reasons. Donna began to volunteer for this duty and to swap shifts with grateful colleagues who had families. In her turn she spent as many nights tucking in male residents as she did sleeping in the staff flat until the owners, and quickly thereafter Barry, found out. She was punished by having to go home each evening to her husband.

Her frustration and anger grew until one night she found herself in the bar with three of the local rugby team who were drunk and abusive. She didn't mind any of that too much but she was sure that none of them were sober enough to perform in bed to her exacting standards. The only other person in the bar that night, was the recently arrived Robbie Buchanan, who had eaten in the restaurant quite late and was alternating his attention between his laptop and Donna's breasts.

The noise of the drunken rugby players got louder and their comments and innuendo grew steadily cruder. The comments developed into coarse suggestion and eventually the largest of the three, Bob 'The Horse' Clydesdale reached over the bar and grabbed Donna's left breast as she turned towards the till. She screamed in genuine fear and surprise and stood back from the counter shouting at Bob to leave and that he was barred. He ignored her and leaned across the counter again with his long right arm.

Robbie had watched closely, as the volume had eventually precluded any chance of continuing to work at his laptop.

When he saw Bob continue his assault he said in a calm but loud voice: "Just leave her and go home."

Bob immediately turned his attention to Robbie who stood up and faced Bob. Bob was six foot five inches tall and weighed over eighteen stone. He had a reputation on the rugby pitch as a vicious bastard even by local standards, who would never dodge a tackle. In the scrum he would taunt his opposite numbers with threats and, safe from television replays at his level of the game, would punch and kick opponents whenever he could.

Robbie on the other hand was just over five foot ten inches tall, weighed about twelve stone and had been seen by the lads limping in from the restaurant after his meal. Bob and his friends sensed some fun and Donna anticipated the need for an ambulance, the police and a difficult meeting with her boss the following morning. She made a sign to Robbie suggesting he forgot the whole thing and left, but he ignored it.

"This is none of your business hop-a-long," slurred Bob and his friends burst out laughing.

"Go home, sunshine," said Robbie. "You've had enough."

Bob laughed again and took two steps toward Robbie. Everyone in the room was aware afterwards that Robbie had then moved and hit Bob, but it had happened so quickly that the exact details were vague, even allowing for the alcohol consumed. Robbie's fist had struck Bob in the solar plexus with the speed and force of a steam piston. Bob sank to his knees as quickly as Robbie grew in Donna's estimation. He tried to get to his feet but his legs had gone and his friends, in a state of shock, quietly helped him up and half carried him out of the bar for safety.

"Thank you Mr Buchanan," said Donna in awe. "There was no need, but I am glad you did that. He has had that coming for years. Can I get you a drink? On the house."

Robbie smiled, ignoring the pain in his fist and opted for a Famous Grouse whisky which, he noticed, arrived as a double measure. If pressed he would have admitted that he had enjoyed hitting the young bully but realised his cover as a researcher into the loss of rare species in the area was looking a bit shaky.

"I used to box at school," he said, "You never really lose it."

He thanked Donna for the drink and tried to re-focus on the pages he had been reading on his laptop. While he failed to achieve that, Donna phoned home and explained to her husband that the live-in member of staff had phoned in sick and she would, reluctantly have to sleep over again. He accepted this as usual and turned back to his computer screen to watch the rather specialist Swedish film he had been watching on a live stream.

When Donna returned to the bar, Robbie noticed that the top two buttons of her blouse appeared to have spontaneously opened of their own volition and her ample chest was even less fettered than usual.

"I really wanted to thank you again for what you did. I've locked the doors just in case they try anything silly. We wouldn't want to be taken by surprise would we?"

Robbie suspected Donna had never been taken by surprise in her life and whether the doors were to keep somebody in or out was highly debateable. He had, however, faced greater dangers than a buxom barmaid and decided he was happy to face this particular threat in the line of duty.

"It would be a pity if anyone caught us unawares," he agreed.

The talk continued in this vain as Donna joined him on the neighbouring bar stool with a double gin and tonic, again on the house. Their gaze met, then their ankles touched, then their hands, their mouths and after a further four hours in the bar and in Robbie's room very little of Robbie remained untouched by any part of Donna.

He had been initially concerned what might be her reaction to his artificial leg. As it turned out he was not sure she had even noticed. He had known many passionate nights, especially in his student days but none as physically taxing as that night with Donna. Eventually they fell asleep or more accurately Donna fell asleep and allowed him to follow suit. The respite was short lived as she woke him up at six in the morning for a deciding match before showering and dressing quickly and leaving him, to sleep again. He missed breakfast but decided that was a very small price to pay for the feast which had gone before.

Over the next week, Robbie found himself spending the night with Donna on two further occasions. Each time the experience was both satisfying and exhausting. His love life had suddenly swung from famine to feast and he had no intention of complaining while it lasted. As before, it lasted until the owners found out and told Donna in no uncertain terms to go home each night at the end of the shift and that the only member of staff authorised to stay overnight in the Hotel was Kevin the chef. Fortunately for Robbie, on this occasion Barry somehow didn't hear about it.

Chapter 15

Robbie and the Treasure Hunters

After five days in the village, Robbie had found himself in a conversation with two locals, David and Clive, who were very keen detectorists. Although he glazed over at first when they began to tell him all about their hobby with an enthusiasm he didn't share, it soon became clear that they both spent a lot of time in the fields and farms around Kirkton. It seemed likely that they would have a good knowledge of the area and perhaps regarding the movements of the locals too. After an hour or so of discussions, Robbie found himself invited to join them on a jaunt the following morning.

It had been a genuine and generous invitation and Robbie decided it might be a good way of learning more about the village, its population and the surrounding area. He didn't altogether fancy trudging any great distance over rough ground but David had assured him that they had clearance from a farmer to go onto some land which was reasonably flat and close to the road.

The following day the weather was dry if not sunny and the fresh air began to brighten everyone after the initial hangovers they had awoken with had worn off. Robbie was handed a metal detector by David who gave him a rudimentary lesson in its use, including the noise to listen for when it passed over a coin. This David demonstrated by throwing a ten pence piece on to the ground beside them.

"Any problems with digging and one of us will give you a hand," said David and Clive nodded his agreement.

Robbie found a few nails initially, unable to tell the difference in tone between them and buried treasure. After an hour or so he heard a sharper buzz from the machine and suspected a better find. Sure enough, when Clive helped him uncover the source of the signal, it turned out to be a two pence piece. Everyone, Robbie included, was elated at the restoration of this coin back into circulation, despite its nominal value.

As the morning wore on, Robbie became aware of an underlying tension between the two enthusiasts, whom he had assumed were the best of friends. It became clear that they were nothing of the kind. They may once have been but now they were rivals and his presence was a rare truce in their spat. As each helped him in turn, they would voice criticisms of the other, which became stronger and more profane as the session progressed across the field. Their meetings in the pubs had been less about shared experiences and more about continuing an argument and checking up on each other's movements. By lunch time, Robbie was rather pleased to be able to return to the Wagon with his dirty two pence piece and reflect on the strange experience of watching two people so distrusting of each other that they spent hours in each other's company. Both had funds to spend on expensive kit and both seemed certain the other had recently made a very valuable find without sharing the information.

"Interesting," he mused, as his ploughman's lunch arrived with a very welcome pint of Guinness.

Chapter 16

Old Bill checks Robbie Out

Sometime after his arrival in Kirkton, Robbie found himself sitting on one of the many benches dotted around Kirkton and which were dedicated to the departed and beloved former members of the community. This particular one was dedicated to one Alan Armitage, (butcher), "who always loved this view". Robbie could see his point and was enjoying the rare sunshine when he saw the large local policeman hove into view. He was in civilian clothes and was walking a dog which Robbie assumed was his own but was realising by now might belong to a neighbour, friend or illicit partner. In the case of the village police sergeant he gave him the benefit of the doubt and ruled out the last option.

"Just walking a friend's dog," said Bill, enigmatically, as he arrived at the bench. "May I join you?"

"Please do," replied Robbie.

"Nice day for a walk," began Old Bill. "How are you getting on with your rare species survey? I gather you have come into contact with a few of our more interesting specimens?"

"You could say that," laughed Robbie. "I am certainly getting a lot of information from your friends and neighbours."

"I'm sure," said Bill. "Although this is not my beat as such I always take a close interest in what goes on here and any new faces as it were. It doesn't take much just to reassure myself that the peace and quiet of Kirkton isn't in danger. There have been a few odd goings-on recently and I thought I better just make sure you were who you said you were. No offence."

"None taken," said Robbie, wondering what was coming next. He knew he had no criminal record, indeed no record at all as Robbie Buchanan, beyond basic checks that the local police might do for driving purposes.

"As you'll be aware all was in order. No criminal records. Just to make certain, I asked a friend of mine in Special Branch, well Counter Terrorist Branch as it is now to run some checks for me to put my mind at rest. Still no offence intended."

"Still none taken."

"Well, you can imagine my surprise when the Chief Superintendent phoned me at home and told me in no uncertain terms to stop sticking my nose into your affairs. He also suggested that I try and give you any assistance I can, especially with local knowledge, and peoples' background. Seemed a bit of overkill to protect our native species, as it were. So between you and me and the late Mr Armitage's ghost; what are you doing here and just what the hell am I meant to help you with, Robbie? Should I call you Robbie, by the way?"

"Robbie's fine," said Robbie. "Even I'm getting used to it now. In terms of how you can help, I'm not able to give too much detail in terms of why I'm here. It involves a lot of money. Cash. I need to know if anyone locally has suddenly started spending large amounts of the stuff."

"What sort of amounts are we talking about?"

"Ultimately very big sums, but locally, any amount which is out of the ordinary. Not the usual folk who always deal in cash, but different people, or maybe the usual suspects with money to burn. I am looking specifically at the last two to three weeks only."

"This community is a wealthy one with some very generous people in it. There is a lot of money about, though not usually large amounts of cash. There are a number of people who do use amounts of cash to buy most things. Vehicles, livestock and a lot of other items connected to work on the land. I am sure there will be a number of such transactions during the timescale you are looking at. I gather the new minister has discovered envelopes with wads of cash in them at the door of the church. We are talking about several thousand pounds in total, but no hint as to who is responsible. It seems to have started around that time too, although the minister himself is new and I don't know if this happened with his predecessor. If it did, I was unaware of it. Not sure if that helps any."

"It may well be something along those lines. The envelopes are interesting; any idea who they might be coming from?"

"None at all. Philanthropy isn't a crime as far as I am aware, so the police haven't been involved. If you tell me whose money it is and that it has been stolen I am all ears."

"I'm afraid I can't divulge that information. Let's just say that your boss and my boss are both very keen to learn where it went and to speak to the person who has it regarding its prompt return."

"I assume no laws will be broken along the way and all parties involved will be operating within the rule of law. I retire very soon and don't want my last few months in the force to see the first serious trouble this area has had since the Battle of Flodden."

"I am sure your Chief Superintendent would not be a party to anything that was outside the law of the land."

Old Bill thought about the conversation with Chief Superintendent Ian Jackson and wasn't so sure. He knew for certain he didn't like being ordered to help a complete stranger in his patch investigate something which may or may not be a crime; a stranger who was definitely not a policeman. This whole talk of missing money bothered him in principle. A lot of his undercover work in Edinburgh had been centred around recouping cash from the drugs trade under the proceeds of crime legislation. He had firmly come to the conclusion that cash was a dangerous commodity in the wrong hands. If it was in his powers, money would always be under the close control of an entirely responsible person, such as a minister, a lawyer or a policeman for example.

"I'll keep my ears to the ground and my eyes open. How do you know the money is in this village?"

"We have good reason to believe it is in the hands of a local resident. Again I can't go into the reasons for that likelihood."

"Well, I'd better be getting Brambles here back to his owner. I'll keep in touch while I'm still here."

"Thanks. Sorry I can't be more open with you."

Bill just shrugged his shoulders as he walked off with the small terrier he was walking for the unspecified friend. There was a hint of resignation in the gesture. Perhaps a hint of impending retirement and a knowledge that soon this would all be someone else's patch and these would all be someone else's problems.

Chapter 17

Billy MacPherson

Billy MacPherson had gone onto Robbie's list very early during his time in Kirkton and stubbornly remained there ever since. Billy had lived in the area for years but was not originally from Kirkton itself. None of the original inhabitants had been at school with him and although the date was vague they agreed amongst themselves that he must have arrived well over twenty years ago as a relatively young man, freshly expelled from Her Majesty's Royal Navy. He had been a heavy drinker when he arrived and there were stories of battles with some of the farmers' lads in the dim and distant past. Peace had broken out however when Billy had decided he liked Kirkton, wanted to stay and that he could achieve that most easily by not fighting everyone in sight when drunk. He was smart enough to recognise in himself the latent ability to settle down, and that it could only be realised by taking the pledge. As a result he had stopped drinking completely and was thereafter one of the few people in the village who was genuinely teetotal. He remained many other things but he was no longer a bar-room brawler, and he had become a stranger to subsequent generations of village policemen. This had been so long ago that Old Bill had never had cause to arrest Billy for drunkenness or indeed anything else, although his name was occasionally mentioned in connection with missing items in the neighbourhood. These rumours were never supported by evidence and it was not impossible that Billy was an entirely law-abiding citizen. Unlikely but not impossible.

He was many things to many people but above all others he was a friend to those in need. If anyone moved into one of the few social housing properties in the village lacking the basics in terms of furniture and household goods then Billy would forage and appeal on their behalf, soon providing the necessities of life. Old ladies could rely on him to rescue cats from trees, fallen trees from their gardens or almost any minor household repair. He would always refuse money but would never refuse a cup of tea or home baking whilst there, or prepared food to take away. This he would reheat later in his one bedroomed council house and feed anyone who dropped in. This could be anything up to twelve people at times, but they would all leave fed. Younger ladies in the area could rely on him for other services not always fulfilled outdoors. Although he was regarded by some as a rogue and sponger he was regarded by others as, if not a saint, then at least a rough diamond. He saw himself as a freelance social worker, happy to work for the meagre level of benefits he received rather than a full salary with the council. It was also true that they would have been as reluctant to employ him as he would have been reluctant to work for anyone full-time. In this state of balance he existed with the local benefits agency, always managing to remain one step ahead of central government attempts to force him into earning an honest living.

His principle skill lay in foraging. Not just furniture and white goods for the needy in the area, but also free food from the surrounding countryside (which for Billy included any unattended gardens). In this respect he was greatly aided by the number of holiday homes in the village. In return for harvesting fruit Billy would often prune and tidy fruit trees and bushes wherever he went. The less charitable in the area might state that this was only in order to achieve a better crop for Billy the following year, but for most it was all part and parcel of his generally altruistic approach to life, the universe, everything. His foraging took him far and wide into all areas of the valley for five miles or so on either side of the village. He knew the best places to find sloes, berries, wild gooseberries, cherries, plums and apples. He knew when each would be ready for picking and which ones to collect first in order to outmanoeuvre the competition. His greatest gift, and the one which earned him raw cash, was the ability to find edible mushrooms, many of which were highly prized by the chefs in the local restaurants. Chanterelle mushrooms in particular could keep Billy in funds for much of the year.

This ability also funded the modest car which was the only luxury he allowed himself. It was an unofficial taxi to many in the area, although the local authority had never managed to prove that money ever changed hands for its services. It could be seen regularly after village functions transporting people home and was so well known, as was Billy, that if the local police were carrying out a random roadside check for drunk drivers they would usually wave it through to save everyone's time. Billy never drank. They knew it, and if he was driving a few people home who were the worse for wear then it was a community service which potentially saved them a job. On some of these occasions, however, the contents of his boot may have proved of more interest to them.

It became evident to Robbie soon after arriving that Billy was a strong contender for finding the missing cash, and he was placed high on the list. Billy moved in mysterious ways, both by day and night, and could easily have seen the stricken helicopter. His forces background would have kicked in, perhaps along with his innate desire to help, and he might have rushed to the scene of its initial struggle when it had to discharge its cargo. If he had been the finder then he would also know where to hide the money; somewhere handy enough but where it would never be found by anybody else. Unfortunately for Robbie, Billy was so successful in shrouding his activities in mystery that he was never able to rule him out or indeed prove any guilt. As a result Billy stayed on his list of subjects as others were deleted one by one.

Chapter 18

An Accommodating Woman

After three weeks at the Wagon, Robbie was informed
by his contact in London that the department would no
longer pick up the tab for him staying in a hotel, and that
he should find cheaper accommodation in the village.
Robbie knew that it was simply Jennifer messing with his
mind because he hadn't found the money yet. The
difference in cost between the hotel and digs in a local
house would be negligible, and would be nothing
compared to the London weighting allowance paid to
even the most junior civil servant there. In truth he was
slightly relieved. He reckoned he had discovered all that
he could from the locals in the Wagon and Donna had
grown rather cold to him of late. Perhaps it was time to
meet more of the villagers than just the pub -going
fraternity. With this in mind he started asking round
about longer-term accommodation in the village and
was pleased to discover from one of the staff at the shop
that a lady by the name of Betty McVicar took in lodgers
and might have an empty room.

"Does she do evening meals too?" asked Robbie.

"I believe she'll do pretty much anything if you're prepared to pay the extra cost," replied the assistant in the shop.

Robbie suspected there might have been a slight giggle in her voice as she said it, and wasn't quite sure if a double entendre was meant. Either way he needed a room, and it sounded as if she had one spare. Jotting down Betty's address and phone number he thanked the assistant and headed out of the shop and back to his room at the Wagon.

"Could I speak to Mrs McVicar, please?" Robbie asked when he phoned the number he had been given.

"Speaking, and it's Ms McVicar, but please call me Betty," Betty corrected him gently.

"My name is Buchanan and I was told at the shop that you might have a room to rent. I am looking for one for two weeks or so, perhaps longer."

"You're in luck Mr Buchanan, or should I call you Robbie? I have one at the moment. I had a BT engineer staying for a few weeks while he worked on the local cabling, but he moved out last week."

Robbie was no longer surprised when people in the village knew his name or most of his business even if he had never met them before. There was an all-informed intelligence network in operation within Kirkton which would have put the Secret Intelligence Service to shame.

"Please call me Robbie. Could I pop over and have a look at the room this morning, although I am sure it will be fine."

"Mr Atkinson the BT engineer found it most satisfactory," replied Betty McVicar, quickly enough to suggest she had taken a little bit of offence at Robbie's requirement to check out her room before committing himself.

"Oh in that case I'll take it for the two weeks initially," countered Robbie, keen not to start off on the wrong foot with the person cooking his meals for the foreseeable future. "I'll bring my things over in an hour or so if that's okay."

Betty confirmed that it would be fine and Robbie hung up. The lady's name didn't appear on any of his lists and he couldn't put a face to it so perhaps this would afford him a whole new set of contacts and a new source of gossip. He packed away his belongings and made his way through to the bar to pay his bill. When he got there he found another new face beside the till, but his bill was ready and waiting for him and the rather heavy middle aged woman asked politely if he had enjoyed his stay.

Robbie confirmed that he had but stopped short of mentioning that he was moving to Ms McVicar's house. There was presumably an etiquette in such things and he didn't know quite how it would be viewed by his recent hosts. He needn't have worried. As he picked up his two pieces of luggage and limped towards the door the lady behind the bar shouted after him, "Betty will look after you just as well."

"That was quick," he thought to himself as he struggled through the front door and put his luggage into the car.

Betty lived in a large mid-terraced property in Little Kirkton which had three letting rooms. Two of them were available on a Bed and Breakfast basis at a rate only slightly below that of the two hotels, while the third tended to have a lodger in as a source of lower but more regular income. Robbie arrived at the house to find Betty McVicar waiting for him on a garden seat at the front of the property. She was a well preserved woman of fifty or so who must have been a real looker in her younger days. She may have carried a bit too much weight now and worn too much lipstick for some people's tastes but she was still an attractive lady. Her summer dress was a little bit too short and flowery in Robbie's opinion but he was there to work, not write a fashion column.

Betty slowly uncrossed her legs, smiled and rose to meet him as his car pulled up in front of the house.

"You are a quick worker, aren't you Robbie?" she asked in a rather teasing way for a first encounter.

"I like to travel light," he answered hoping there were no double meanings in anything he said.

"I'll show you the room and then help you with your things."

Betty led the way up the stairs of the house with her dress swinging about alluringly in front of Robbie's face. He tried to avert his eyes but quickly gave up. At the first landing Betty turned right and showed him into a large bedroom which had a tiny ensuite shower room crammed into a corner. The bed was a king size and was tastefully covered in Laura Ashley covers. Betty pointed out all the key aspects of the room, including the kettle and drinks-making facilities, the shower room and the reading lights beside the bed. She then went over to the window and explained that it boasted an excellent view. When Robbie turned towards it he found her leaning unnecessarily far over the deep window ledge at the garden, a position which afforded him an excellent view of the tops of her thighs. He turned away quickly and looked into the shower room to avoid any embarrassment. Betty turned round and seemed disappointed to find him staring at the heat controls of the shower.

"It's a lovely room," said Robbie hoping to be left alone.

Instead Betty sat on the bed and smoothed an imaginary crease from the cover.

"This is a very comfy bed," she said. "Nice and roomy."

"It looks very comfortable," agreed Robbie. "I'm sure I will sleep very well in it."

"It could tell a tale or two," continued Betty.

"Several volumes from your memoirs alone," thought Robbie to himself but said nothing.

After a short pause Betty offered to help bring his luggage up.

"I'll be fine thank you, Mrs..."

"Betty. Please let me help. I try to make the stay as relaxing as possible and I couldn't help noticing your limp. I hope you don't mind me mentioning it?"

"No it's fine," said Robbie hoping against hope that she would leave him alone. She was a bit too keen to show him round the bedroom for his liking. In the end he decided it might save time if he let her bring up the luggage and then he could make an excuse to stay in the room alone and sort it.

Betty jumped at the chance to be useful and disappeared downstairs to fetch the two items from the back of Robbie's car. He breathed a sigh of relief and switched the shower on to suggest he would be using it as soon as he could.

When Betty returned with his luggage, she was sweating slightly from the effort and flapped the top of her dress gently to allow the air to circulate. More flesh was exposed at the same time and Robbie failed to look away in time.

"I thought I would take a shower before going out," he said quickly.

"I'm sweating so much after climbing the stairs with your bags I almost need to join you," said Betty suggestively.

Robbie hesitated for a second before adding, "I think I'd better just use the shower myself, if that's okay."

After a pause, Betty laughed as if her comments had all been in jest, and left Robbie alone.

Robbie sighed a sigh of relief and locked his door quietly. Then he had a shower, dressed and went out of the bed and breakfast without encountering Betty again.

Over the next few days the pattern of cat and mouse continued. Betty seemed adept at finding reasons to be in Robbie's room and he was a poor second at finding reasons for her to leave. She would make suggestive remarks and he would reply politely till she would eventually and reluctantly leave him alone. Although the offer of evening meal was there (amongst much else), he preferred to eat in the two hotels alternately to try and finish his mission and find the missing money. Despite his initial reluctance to spend time with Betty, he had to make arrangements for meals etc. and would be forced to seek her out on occasions. It was during one of these searches that he knocked on the door of the spare room besides Betty's and looked in. He found himself staring at a folding bed, not unlike the kind you might find in a doctor's examination room. It had a neat pile of towels on it and there were more on a sideboard against the wall with a range of massage oils, both perfumed and unperfumed.

"Curious," he thought to himself before quietly closing the door again and making his way to his own bedroom.

As the days passed since he left the Wagon and the memories of Donna's friendly welcome to the village faded he found himself thinking more and more about the massage table and Betty's constant insistence on how important it was to relax while under her roof. The BT engineer's stay was a recurring theme at the breakfast table and on the occasions when a lonely

Robbie found himself having a nightcap in Betty's sitting room before retiring for the night.

"How relaxed was he?" he wondered. "Perhaps it's best just to speculate on that one."

During the daytime he covered as much of the countryside around the electricity pylon as his disability would allow. He wasn't entirely sure what he was looking for, but it tied in with his cover and gave him the feeling of doing something useful. He didn't really expect to find the money or the guilty party on his walks but he felt better in his mind for keeping busy. His body didn't feel better though; anything but. By the end of some days, despite the regular consumption of several drinks in one of the two hotels he would find himself in considerable pain. Not just pains at the stump of his leg but in all the other muscles of his lower body which were overcompensating as he forced them to cover the ground. He was used to pain from his athletics career and from his training with MI6. In both sets of circumstances it had taken a lot before it hurt. Nowadays a few miles seemed like a marathon with a rucksack on.

On one such evening he almost collapsed into the chair in Betty's sitting room. She noticed the look of pain in his face and brought a large glass of whisky over without asking if he wanted it or not. He thanked her and took a swallow to try to ease the aches across his hips and buttocks. As the drink joined the others in his system he began to relax and found himself staring at Betty as she watched television. One of her favourite soap operas was on and she had managed to focus her attention on it rather than her male lodger for once. He looked at her profile against the velvet curtain. Then his gaze fell to her full breasts and onward to her hips. Suddenly she looked round and caught his eye as he tried to look away, but it was too late.

"I am a trained exponent of herbal massage. Perhaps I could help ease the pains in your legs? Your leg, I mean. Whatever hurts."

"Is that an alternative therapy? I've tried most things."

"Try this alternative of mine. I guarantee you'll forget about the pain. Promise."

Robbie stared at her and thought about the massage table he had seen. He thought about how happy and relaxed the BT engineer had been by all accounts. He thought about the freshly laundered towels. He thought about the oils, both perfumed and unperfumed that he had seen on the sideboard. As he stood up and followed Betty slowly upstairs he found that the pain had already started to fade. Somehow he knew that she was right and that soon he would forget the pain entirely.

Chapter 19

Pub Quiz

The Wagon hotel was the centre of life for many who enjoyed a drink in Kirkton itself. The darts team met and drank on a Friday, the pool team on a Tuesday, the bridge club in the restaurant on a Thursday, and the domino club whenever two or more were present. Many people belonged to more than one of the groups, with the exception of the bridge club, none of whom played darts, pool or dominos. Despite this, most members of most clubs were on at least nodding terms with the others, including the bridge club. Only the monthly pub quiz united all sections of the community in shared competition. In theory it was a regular bit of fun to raise money for local causes and as such gave non-regulars an excuse to be seen in a public house. In practice, however, it was a life-and-death struggle between three of the regular teams, with no quarter sought or given. Not only was there genuine animosity between teams during the evenings and sometimes beyond, but the answers and scoring were scrutinised to ensure every possible chance of winning was grabbed. The

135

quizmaster's evenings could be bruising occasions where they had to be prepared to justify each answer against arguments from several teams (which included at least two lawyers and many retired teachers). As a result only a few people of the thickest of thick skin and resolve were prepared to undertake the task. Many had tried in the past and many had fallen by the wayside, unable to soak up the pressure and vitriol. It was therefore always welcome when a newcomer to the village volunteered to set a quiz. This gave the usual quizmasters a well-earned rest, but as it also gave them the opportunity to take part, they were eagerly sought after by one or more of the more competitive teams.

When Robbie offered to run one of the quizzes he was surprised at how quickly the offer was taken up. Initially he saw it as an opportunity to get to know the villagers he hadn't already met. Donna had joked that he must be really brave or foolish when she heard and Robbie had beamed with pride. It was only after a few people had approached him for hints as to the subject areas he had in mind, usually buying him a drink first, that he realised it might not be as simple a task as he had at first thought. When others told tales of alleged match fixing and favouritism in the past he began to get a feeling for how seriously the event was taken. His original plan had been to get to know a wider range of locals than he had managed to date, in the friendly atmosphere of a charity event. It now might be possible to view a large gathering of the villagers at their most basic level. In these circumstances it might be easier to spot someone who had recently gained vast wealth and was careless about letting it show. Either way, Robbie was committed to running the quiz to raise funds for the local single mothers club whether he liked it or not. To pull out now would be to show cowardice in the face of the enemy in a way he could never have justified to himself.

He had spent a lot of time on the internet, not only coming up with what he thought were three well balanced rounds of questions but also checking and double-checking the answers. To make sure he could deal with any query from the teams he also wrote down some notes beside each answer to justify what he would and would not accept. Finally, he came up with four tie-breaker questions just in case he had been unable to separate the teams during the main rounds. All in all he arrived at the Wagon on the appointed hour confident that he would succeed where others had failed and that every team would leave feeling that they had taken part in a fair quiz with no grounds for complaint.

As he looked round the lounge bar at the teams, nodding at the locals he knew, he noticed that there were a large number of faces that he didn't recognise at all. Some smiled but many others simply stared at him in a way that suggested this was too serious for smiles and that as quiz master he was the foe. The lady with the bright dyed red hair was sitting in a corner with a different man again and they formed an intimate team of their own. He also noticed that David and Clive were now in different teams, teams which he recognised as being bitter rivals.

The first round was designed to be an easy start for all concerned with some questions on traditional school subjects of geography, history, maths, physics and chemistry. He had called it 'Back to School' and hoped the team of retired teachers would approve. Sadly they simply pointed out three spelling errors as the quiz sheets were handed out before focusing on what they certainly found to be an easy round. The other teams huddled round the sheets and discussed the answers in hushed tones. This gave Robbie a chance to study the faces of those who were still on his list of possibles and, in particular, David and Clive.

He noticed that each of them regularly looked over at the other but immediately looked away if their gazes met. The hostility between them was palpable. Robbie knew that each one now distrusted the other and that both had invested heavily in new metal detectors recently. Both had also spent money on a new car too. It was hardly conclusive proof in either case, but Robbie had little else to go on. If an opportunity arose to catch either of them out he would grab it and hopefully see guilt in the eyes of one of them. Whether tonight would provide such an opportunity or not he did not know, but he kept a close watch on them both just in case.

His attention, however, was soon largely taken up by the quiz itself as he became embroiled in the bitter team rivalry and combative attention to detail he had been warned about. After the unfortunate start of typing errors being pointed out by the team of retired teachers things continued downwards with a query about one of the answers in his geography section. The capital of the Netherlands was Amsterdam he had confirmed. Someone immediately countered that it was The Hague as it was the seat of government, held the Council of State and also the Supreme Court. Robbie was ready for this, however, and from his notes argued that Amsterdam was enshrined as the capital in the constitution of The Netherlands dated 1588 because it was a royal city where the monarch was crowned and where royalty got married. Expecting this to end the argument he was surprise when the elderly lady with the blue rinse came back at him with a simple 'Bollocks' and turned back to her team.

Round two had been a small general knowledge round and here too there was controversy over the question of what constituted a sardine. He had written down "a young herring" on his answer sheet and beside it "bonus point for the small oily young of various members of Clupeidae/part of the herring family". Nobody claimed the available bonus point.

There was a snort from the same blue rinsed lady as before who shouted out "they are young pilchards" in a way that suggested everyone knew that. This time it was echoed by a few others and Robbie looking down at his notes with relief noticed a few lines.

"Pilchards are sardines larger than six inches but all are members of the Clupeidae genus, a branch of the herring family," said Robbie. "A half mark for pilchards, then."

Another snort from the direction of the blue rinse suggested this was not the judgement of Solomon Robbie had hoped it might be.

Other queries to answers followed in each round and he was glad he had done his homework and taken notes. He was also thrown by the fact that every round had to be scored and the winner announced, as there was a prize for each. Nobody had thought to mention this to him and he was forced to use his tie-breaker questions after round one. The format was that each team nominated a team member to stand in front of Robbie who asked the tie-break question. Whoever answered first won the round for their team.

Robbie had found two serious-looking team members approach him after it was realised their teams had tied for round one. It was quickly explained to him what he had to do. He pulled his tie-breaker sheet from his pocket and looked at the first question. He had been quite proud of it and felt it would be appreciated, including as it did a local reference.

"What name is shared by a borders rugby ground and a novel by Jane Austen?"

To his surprise both the nominated team champions answered in unison that it was Mansfield Park and the whole room groaned as if he had asked the most obvious question in the universe. A little flustered, he turned to the next question on his sheet.

"How many men have walked on the moon?"

After a pause, one of the retired teachers correctly answered 12, to everyone's relief, especially Robbie's.

The quiz continued in this way, until all rounds were completed and Robbie retired to a corner to total up the scores while the raffle was drawn. Although he had no idea which team had won, three of the other teams had already calculated that two teams were drawn for first place and that yet another tie-break would be needed. Discussion took place within these teams so that when Robbie stood up to announce the fact he was faced with the nominated champions from each team. Robbie was further thrown by the fact that David and Clive had been chosen.

Recovering quickly he had a sudden thought. As the two rivals reluctantly lined up beside each other to face him Robbie announced that he would now ask the tie-break question to decide the winning team for the evening. David and Clive faced him and focused intently on his mouth, seeking any possible advantage they could gain.

Robbie stared at them in the hush of the room and whispered: "Which one of you found the money?"

David looked puzzled by this strange tie-break question but Clive's jaw dropped with a guilty reflex action. "Got you!" thought Robbie, staring at Clive who was trying desperately to recover his composure.

"Just kidding," whispered Robbie to the confused figures in front of him before asking in a loud voice: "Who played The Man with the Golden Gun in the James Bond film of that name?"

David was quicker to the draw and answered 'Christopher Lee' to win the quiz for his team, while Clive was left floundering and trying to understand what had just happened. Although David had won the quiz he was now staring at Clive with a scowl which could have curdled milk and the two former friends walked back to their respective teams eyeing daggers at each other all the way.

"Result," though Robbie as he returned to the bar after polite applause thanked him for his efforts during the night.

"You did well tonight," remarked Donna as she handed him a beer on the house. "There is usually a lot more arguing and foul language. Even Nessie Jones was on her best behaviour. That was her with the blue rinse."

Robbie smiled a smile of relief as he started to slowly unwind after the stress of running his first pub quiz at the Wagon. He had felt it to be a bruising encounter throughout, but Donna's honest expression suggested he had achieved a better than average result. From his point of view though, the real result had been the look of obvious guilt in Clive's face. "The quiz is the thing wherein I'll catch the conscience of the king," he mused, feeling as if he had somehow acquired supreme knowledge of all things.

A quick email to his contact in London afterwards led to a mysterious break-in at Clive's house the following day. No bundles of dollars or pounds were found, but the search team did uncover a metal box containing almost 2,000 ancient Scottish silver coins, well hidden under a floor board in the spare bedroom. Instructions in their earpieces ordered them to leave it where it was. Thereafter Clive had the curious feeling of being watched for weeks after the break-in without being able to pin down why.

Chapter 20

A favour for the President

President George Jesus Emanuel Thackery was the first US President with Hispanic origins and as such understood poverty and the desire to create a better life for oneself and one's family. He didn't understand poverty from personal experience of course, but he had relatives who were quite poor and some of them had friends and neighbours who were dirt poor. Fortunately for him he also had relatives on the Boston side of the family with money - serious money - and that had allowed him to go through fee -paying schools and straight into Yale. This side of the family had allowed his early dreams of political office to become a reality. The memories of the other side of his family stayed with him, though, on the campaign trail and he saw in the many disadvantaged people he met throughout his political career something approaching kindred spirits. If he could become President of the USA with just a little help along the way, then a little help from him could perhaps allow others to fulfil their own destinies. This formalised into a personal policy whereby he tasked one of his junior researchers to identify people of ability wherever he visited, who lacked the opportunity to take the first steps to advancement for themselves or their families. The policy was not confined to his domestic tours. If he visited any foreign lands he would try to help a few of the locals too. Once identified, these individuals and their immediate families would be scrubbed up and brought under high security to a private audience with President Thackery. There he would take the time to speak to them and, helped by the notes from his researcher and one of his closest advisers, identify a way to give them a helping hand.

This was a personal commitment which he took very seriously and kept private and out of the hands of his PR team. They were aware of it and jealously watched photo-opportunity after photo-opportunity pass them by, but they knew anyone breaking the code of secrecy around the Presidents 'Leg-up' activities would be fired.

Thus it was that some of America's brightest but poorest families found a chosen member receiving a scholarship to a prestigious college or the funds to start the business they had always dreamed of.

When the President had paid a surprise visit to US troops in Iraq just before Thanksgiving in his fifth year in office he knew that included in his tight schedule was a full half hour alone (except for twelve secret service guards) with a former doctor of medicine and his family. The doctor had been working as an interpreter for the US forces and knew that when they left, not only would he be unable to return to his practice in Basra, but also his life would be in danger if he stayed in Iraq at all. This he had accepted along with the well-paid job, but his family now faced the same dangers as a result of his work. He had voiced his fears in a letter to the US commander in the Gulf who had passed it through various hands to the Pentagon where it had been forwarded to a presidential aide who happened to be the researcher for 'Leg-up' at that time. She had included it in her weekly meeting and the president had insisted that he personally helped the doctor and his family.

And thus after briefly eating turkey with troops, throwing horseshoes and sitting on a well-guarded tank he was shown into a bomb-proof briefing room where Dr Khalid Hussain and his family were waiting nervously. The president breezed into the room and took Dr Khalid by the hand as if they had known each other all their lives.

"It is a pleasure to meet you, Doctor Khalid, and to get the chance to thank you personally for the work you've being doing for us here."

"The honour is mine," said Dr Khalid who turned and introduced the rest of his family to a president who was enjoying the relaxation of being out of the gaze of the press and to be able to be himself for a change. From the file he had been handed on the flight over he knew the work which Dr Khalid had done for the past six years and the bravery he had shown. He knew that he had received death threats and his family had had to be moved inside the Green Zone for their safety too. Dr Khalid's married daughter was a talented artist but found her work destroyed wherever it was displayed. Her husband was also subject to threats and abuse. Dr Khalid's other two sons were bright and wanted to go to university. Tariq, his older son of twenty, wanted to follow his father's footsteps into medicine but was too much at risk to study in Iraq. Tariq was a good looking lad who was easily distracted by the many girls whose attention he caught. Dr Khalid could see the dangers of keeping him cooped up in a very westernised neighbourhood. The president felt for their plight and had decided to assist them to resettle in the United States, with new identities if necessary.

"I have been told of the dangers you face here and wondered if there was anything I could do for you. I promise to help you in any way I can. This is not just the promise of a politician, but a real promise," Thackery laughed and the family joined in nervously.

"I must move my family somewhere safe. I do not mind staying but please take my wife, sons and my daughter along with her husband to safety."

"I promise you that I will arrange a new life for you in America, where you can make a fresh start. After what you have done here for us, it is the least I can do," and President Thackery smiled his best vote-winning smile.

Dr Khalid looked embarrassed and troubled. "I would like to take my family to a small village somewhere in Britain."

The president maintained his smile through years of practice on the campaign trail.

"Why do you want to go to Britain and not to America?"

"I want my family to live somewhere without guns. Somewhere they can be truly safe from the dangers they have faced here."

The president kept his composure. He had made them a promise and was not one to welch on a deal even with someone who had just slighted his country.

"I think you will find America a very safe place," he countered. "We have some of the best law enforcement officers in the world. You have heard of the FBI too, I take it?"

"Yes, Mr President, and all of these fine people carry guns. As do the CIA, the DEA, US Marshalls, your border guards, your coastguards and the security guards in your supermarkets. We have seen so many guns here, and I have witnessed first-hand what they can do. So now, Mr President, can you help my family move to Britain?"

President Thackery considered continuing with his line of argument but was acutely aware that two days previously a disgruntled postal worker in Ohio had taken three of his five legally-held firearms with him on his rounds. By the time he shot himself he had also shot five dogs and their owners. It was a small incident in a small state but he could do without trying to defend US gun laws here and now. He would have enough difficulty doing that when he got back to Capitol Hill the following day.

"I have made you a promise and I intend to keep it, if humanly possible."

He shook the hands of Dr Khalid and his family before exiting the room surrounded by his body guard, suddenly in a foul mood, Thanksgiving or no Thanksgiving. He indicated to his personal aide who dealt with 'Leg-up' issues that she should come over for instructions.

"Get me the cell phone number of the senior CIA liaison guy in London. Now!"

Twenty minutes later Brad Dexter had got a call on his mobile phone from the President of the United States himself, and the president was in a very bad mood.

Chapter 21

Mr and Mrs Crawley of Croydon

Walter and Roberta Crawley had been visiting the caravan site in Kirkton for over twenty years. Although they had modestly paid jobs in local government and had raised three children, who all went on to graduate from various universities, they had managed to afford one luxury all that time. They had kept a roadworthy caravan for their trips north each school holiday. This also required them to have a large car capable of towing it from Croydon to the Scottish Borders and back each time. With spare cash being non-existent most of this time, Walter and Roberta had had to become proficient mechanics to keep down the costs and they slowly got to know every scrap yard in the Greater London area.

They had first come across Kirkton after taking a wrong turn on the way home from a holiday in Dunbar. Long before satnavs had been thought of they had been using their ten year old road map of the British Isles to visit the four Border abbeys on the way. Later they would debate for hours whose fortuitous mistake it been but they found themselves on a back road rather than a main road, and after several miles arrived at Kirkton. The original plan had been to travel much further that day before stopping at a caravan site but there was something about the feel of the place and the welcome they were given at the petrol station and the village shop which persuaded them to stay the night at the local site. From that night onwards they planned their holidays round the annual sojourn in Kirkton. The parents loved the walking to be had in the valley and surrounding hills. The children loved paddling in the Rowent or fishing with small nets on sticks. As time went by they got to know the local families and felt as if they were going home each time rather than on holiday.

When the children were older and had left home, Walter and Roberta continued to visit Kirkton several times a year, leaving the caravan there during the summer months for ease. It had almost gone without saying that they would retire there when the time came.

Shortly before Walter's sixtieth birthday Roberta's one guilty secret, her single weekly lottery ticket, contained five numbers and the bonus ball. Her heart nearly stopped as she checked the numbers online. Soon afterwards in a state of shock and disbelief she telephoned the claim number to have it confirmed that she had won exactly £479,567. Some people might have been slightly disappointed at not winning the jackpot of over £4 million, but having counted the pennies all her married life, Roberta was ecstatic at the prospect of being able to count £479,567 of her own.

The next thing was the difficult task of telling Walter that she had managed to spend £1 per week since the lottery began without telling him. It felt like a major betrayal as they had always shared everything together and been 100% honest on every subject throughout their marriage, at least as far as she was aware. The feeling of guilt was starting to spoil the enjoyment of the life-changing win. As a result she decided to come clean that evening after tea and before going to collect the cheque. She prepared Walter's favourite meal and risked a glass of red wine for each of them along with it, even though it was Sunday and they both had work the next day.

Walter raised an eyebrow at the sight of the full wine glass beside his placemat and became more suspicious when he saw a plate of mince and mashed potatoes appear from the kitchen, carried by Roberta wearing her best dress and some make-up.

"My luck's in tonight," he thought, and smiled at her as she put the plates onto the table and sat down opposite him.

"I have something to tell you, Walter," she began nervously. "It's something of a confession."

Walter could see how nervous his wife was and his imagination began to run riot. Was she having an affair? Was it with that Bret Fortescue at work? Had she secretly harboured desires for a more adventurous sex life? Perhaps a sex life involving some kinky new fetish. Had she written off the car and they would have to postpone their next trip north? Her long pause confirmed that something big was about to be exposed in their life.

"I have been playing the lottery each week without telling you," she managed to gasp out and then waited for a reaction from Walter.

Walter stared at her deflated. He had built up his hopes that something was about to happen to wreck the mundane existence of their marriage. A separation or a launch into adventurous kinky sex would have been equally acceptable. The actual revelation was, therefore, a complete let-down. So much so that he got quite angry and retorted, "So what, so have I."

He immediately regretted it as he realised the admission of guilt had shocked and hurt his wife.

"I'm sorry, dear," he continued trying desperately to recover the situation. "I should have told you. I always hoped I would win and could surprise you with a new caravan and car at the door and the chance to retire early and take off. To Kirkton, of course. Was there anything else you wanted to say? Please, go on."

"Forget it," said Roberta with a smile and returned to her mince and mash. She savoured each sip of wine as she drank it and even poured a second glass for each of them, an unheard-of extravagance on a Sunday evening. She had plans to make and had to make them alone for now. Later that evening in bed, they made love for a full fifteen minutes before sleeping, another unknown extravagance, with Monday morning looming.

The next day Roberta phoned in sick for the first time in years. She was not in fact ill, and hated lying to anyone, least of all a colleague, but she had arranged to collect her winnings that day and needed to do so without anyone knowing, least of all Walter. A car was dispatched for her from the administration centre of the lottery in the hope that she could be persuaded to allow them to use publicity about her win in their adverts. It wasn't a jackpot win but they had found fewer winners ready to go public of late, and anyone smiling whilst holding an outsize cheque could be useful.

Roberta had insisted on complete anonymity and no amount of free champagne could change her mind. Despite the much-publicised cheques, the funds were paid into her personal account by automated payment and showed as cleared funds before she had left the building. As a result, when she went home mid-afternoon she was able to browse online for a range of items and order them immediately without a hint of guilt or hesitation. She had a detailed plan and was sticking to it. She found the experience exhilarating and exciting simultaneously. By the time Walter came home that evening to see how she was, aware from an email that she had not been at work, everything was ready. Roberta returned to work the following day and surprised all of her colleagues by both the speed of her apparent recovery and by handing in her resignation.

On the Friday she again stayed at home. Her phone call to the office was less sympathetically received than the call on Monday had been and when asked the reason for her absence she paused and said: "You choose." For her part she had a day of serious shopping planned. Shopping with a hire-car and driver to take her where she needed to go, and a professional consultant on hand to advise her.

When Walter returned home that evening he was surprised to find his wife already there with a new and rather short dress on. The table was set for dinner and a wine cooler with a bottle of expensive champagne was sitting in the middle of the table beside a pair of designer crystal glasses. More surprising was the liveried waiter ready to serve it and the smells of exotic cuisine emanating from the kitchen without his wife's presence.

Roberta kissed him passionately on the lips and almost ripped the jacket of his back.

"I've prepared a little surprise for you," she whispered in his ear before biting it.

"So I see," said a dumbstruck Walter and in more than a little pain.

"But let's eat first. Are you hungry?"

"Just a tad," replied Walter trying desperately to make sense of the situation.

"Champagne," she said to the waiter who expertly opened the bottle and poured two glasses.

Roberta threw herself down onto the couch and as she did so the short summer dress rose up revealing a sexy ensemble of stockings, suspenders and crotch less lace panties. Again Walter was dumbstruck, as was the waiter who had thought he had seen it all before. Mind you, he hadn't seen all of Roberta before. The waiter, who answered to the name of Pierre but may have been from Peckham originally, quickly recovered his composure and brought the glasses of Champagne over on a silver tray. As he passed a glass first to Roberta and then to Walter he didn't quite manage to avert his eyes from the lady of the house's legs.

Walter was still a little confused but he was intrigued enough to go along with his wife's plans for the evening. Considering what she was almost wearing underneath her dress the night was full of more promise than any Friday night had been for a very long time. He decided that even if she had lost her senses completely and needed to be institutionalised for life, he could wait until the morning to make the necessary arrangements.

When the champagne was finished the couple made their way to the table where Roberta was assisted into her seat by Pierre. He then opened another bottle of wine from the sideboard and poured a sample amount into one of the glasses in front of Walter. Roberta indicated for him to try it which he did, imitating Oz Clarke from a programme he had watched recently. He knew very little about quality wine but he knew that he had just sampled one. He gave the thumbs up to Pierre who filled Roberta's glass and then topped up Walter's.

Pierre then disappeared into the kitchen and returned two minutes later with a plate of melba toast and some pate de fois gras. Then he retired to the kitchen to allow the couple to enjoy the starter in peace.

Walter was about to say something but his wife put her finger to her lips and whispered: "Just enjoy the meal for now. All will be revealed in due course; and I mean all."

Walter looked again at his wife and, now that she was sitting opposite him at the table noticed for the first time that not only was her dress very short but it displayed rather a lot of cleavage. Cleavage which had not been so well and expensively supported for years. Again his thoughts turned to the possibility of madness, but he was enjoying the evening too much to spoil it early, and simply smiled as he raised his glass and bit into the first piece of toast and pate. It was delicious. On a good Friday they might splash out on a decent Indian or Chinese take away as a treat, but this was a quantum leap beyond that. Pierre appeared twice during the first course to top up the wine glasses and to inquire if everything was to their satisfaction. Both confirmed that it was and Pierre bowed graciously, taking in Roberta's ample bosom as he did so.

When they had both finished, Pierre cleared away both the plates and the wine glasses, much to Walter's initial disappointment. He perked up again though when a new bottle of expensive-looking red wine was opened and a sample poured into the other wine glass at his place for him to assess. Walter had no idea what the wine was but he knew it was the best red he had ever tasted on a

Friday night, at home, in his life. He nodded his approval and again Pierre poured a glass for Roberta before topping up Walter's glass to the brim.

He then went to the kitchen before returning with a French chef in immaculate whites pushing a catering trolley complete with spirit cooker. As Walter watched in amazement the chef expertly prepared two huge steaks to the couple's individual tastes, well done for Roberta and medium rare for Walter himself. In the background Pierre tossed a salad while adding various dressings as the steaks were flambéed by the chef. Walter expected the smoke detector to go off but noticed that the battery for it was lying on top of the side board beside the wine. Impressed, he noticed that Pierre replaced it before leaving that evening. "What a pro," he thought to himself.

Pierre served the steaks and salad before topping up the wine glasses, then he retired again to the kitchen. From time to time he returned to top up wine glasses but otherwise was the soul of discretion. Walter again opened his mouth to ask something but again his wife put her finger to her lips and shushed him.

The steak was the best Walter had ever had, bar none, and he felt the wine complemented it as perfectly as if an expert had put the two together specially. When they had finished Pierre appeared as if by magic and cleared the table. Once he had finished, the chef appeared with a baked Alaska which he himself served before both he and Pierre returned to the kitchen. It was again superb and Walter had given up asking or wondering what was going on in his own house. He knew that his wife was mad, but the symptoms were delicious and he had no intention of stopping things till the night had run its course.

Again when they had finished, Pierre appeared and cleared the table. He opened a bottle of 16 year old Ard Beg and poured a gentleman's measure into a crystal glass for Walter. For Roberta, he poured a large glass of Bailey's over ice. After asking if there was anything else he could do for them he returned to the kitchen.

Roberta stood up, with a little wobble, again revealing large quantities of leg and cleavage and whispered to Walter, "I'll just deal with the staff so we can be alone."

She went through to the kitchen and after a pause of ten minutes or so returned to the table. While she sat down Pierre, the chef and a middle aged lady who had been dealing with the dishes throughout left via the back door into a waiting taxi. Each of them had a tip of one hundred pounds as a thank-you as well as their agency pay to look forward to. Pierre reflected that although it was not the largest tip he had ever received it was generous for the work involved. It was also the first time he had had such a tip pushed down the front of his trousers rather than into his pocket. It was a unique and not unpleasant experience.

The lady turned to them both as the taxi pulled away and said, "Lottery winners?"

"Undoubtedly," replied Pierre as the taxi headed off into the night.

Back in the house Roberta took Walter by the arm and steered him unsteadily towards the front door. As she opened it Walter looked out and was surprised to see that somebody had parked a brand new caravan and Range Rover Vogue in front of their house. "Bloody cheek," he thought.

From the side of the Range Rover a salesman appeared and walked up the pathway.

"Mr Crawley?" he enquired.

"Yes," said Walter.

"Here are the keys for your new car and caravan. I hope you will be very happy with them both."

He handed two sets of keys to Walter and winked briefly at Roberta before heading off into the night.

"What's going…" Walter started to ask but again he was silenced by his wife who led him back into the house by the front of his trousers.

She sat him down on the sofa and kneeled beside him, one hand on his knee, the other on his crotch.

"I have a confession to make to you, Walter. I have been a naughty girl. A very naughty girl indeed and when I tell you what I have done you may spank me if you wish."

Walter was suddenly paying his wife full attention for the first time in years. Aroused and intrigued in equal measure he waited for whatever revelation was next on the evening's agenda.

He managed to whisper: "I most certainly will."

"I have handed in my notice at the council," Roberta confessed.

Walter's jaw dropped but he said nothing.

"I have also been playing the lottery for years and recently won just under half a million pounds. On the basis of that I have typed out a letter of resignation for you to post on Monday from home instead of going to work. I have also arranged for us to drive to Kirkton on Monday where we will be met by an estate agent who will show us round all the houses for sale in the area, all of which we can now afford to buy for cash. I have been reliably informed that our house here would rent out for £2,000 per month after costs. That should allow us to be very comfortable for the rest of our lives."

She then stood up and walked towards the sideboard with an accentuated swinging of her hips which caused the dress to rise up as she walked. There she picked up a large cigar and walked back to the table.

Walter was a non-smoker, as much through economy as choice, but in his younger days he had thoroughly enjoyed the occasional cigar. He had never before smoked such a choice Cuban cigar as his wife had in her hand. Nor had anyone used a twenty pound note to light one for him from a candle before. As she pushed the cigar into his open mouth she whispered, "For the first time in our lives we now have money to burn. I intend to carry a lot of cash from now on and to spend, spend, spend."

She pushed Walter onto the couch and then lay across his knees. "If you are really angry you must spank me. Spank me hard on my panties."

Walter reluctantly put down his cigar after taking a long, satisfying puff.

"Oh, I think I will have to. Then I might take you to my room and discuss how things will be from now on. Now that we have every day to ourselves without interruption."

"Oh, I love it when you are so masterful," simpered Roberta. "You may have to punish me often from now on. Especially when we have moved to the countryside and have a secluded garden."

He looked down at both his wife's bottom and the cigar smouldering in the ashtray on the coffee table. In the circumstances he felt morally obliged to leave the cigar smouldering for the moment. "What a waste," he thought as his hand fell on his wife's bottom with a loud slap. This was an evening of lavish spending and wild erotic passions. Two floodgates in his wife had burst open with the lottery win, and the future, like her bottom, was starting to look decidedly rosy.

Chapter 22

Morgana Robertson – The Merry Widow

Morgana Robertson was a wealthy widow who lived in the old manse in Little Kirkton. The house itself had belonged to the family of her late husband Dr Robert Robertson since it had been sold by the Church of Scotland in 1910. She was herself the only child of wealthy farmers and had inherited their money when they died. As a result of the extensive wealth on both sides of the marriage she ended up as the wealthiest person in the village by a huge margin. She was a modest and charitable person by nature and wore her riches lightly. As she walked to the village shop pulling a battered old shopping trolley behind her there was little evidence of millions held in property, stocks, shares and investment accounts. The village knew she had a bob or two, but only a few had any inkling as to the vast amounts involved. She dressed in clothes which would have cost a lot when new, but that had been a long time ago in most cases. Behind the scenes, though, she donated to a wide range of causes close to her heart, including personally funding several local clubs and charities. All of it was done through her solicitors, Messrs Young, Burkett, Young and Elliot. All funding was done in the name of clients of this firm. Her own personal lawyer, Mr Young senior, who was the third generation of his family to work for the firm, carried out all the necessary work involved. He held a weekly meeting with Morgana which would start in the old manse and progress to a conclusion in either the Reiver or the Wagon in turn.

There were even rumours of a romance between the two. For casual observers this was an easy mistake to make. The two were of a similar age. Morgana had been widowed young without children and Mr Young senior had never married. The couple were very comfortable, almost intimate in each other's company. They kissed on the cheek when they met and again when they parted and were clearly very fond of each other. But any idea of physical romance was ill-founded and they remained the best of friends within the confines of a lawyer, client relationship.

Morgana was good company to more than just her legal advisor and was a popular dinner guest in a huge range of social situations. She dined regularly with the two local dukes amongst others, not for her wealth but because of her wit and mischievous sense of humour. She was also a regular guest in the manses of most local villages and any house of note within a twenty mile radius. It was even an open secret that she would pop in for a cup of tea every now and then at Billy MacPherson's house where she would mix effortlessly with his regular band of friends and associates.

The old manse itself was an Aladdin's cave of treasures accumulated by three generations of two wealthy families who had travelled the world. Had anyone carried out a detailed inventory and valuation they would probably have doubled Morgana's estimated net worth. At first sight there were no grand masters' paintings on display. No Turners or Constables or Canaletto's. A closer look, however would discover a Stubbs and several other lesser known British and overseas artists. None of them were worth more than a million individually but every room was decorated beautifully with appropriate pictures and ornaments. The china in the dining room was tastefully selected from some of the best manufacturers over the centuries. Not many houses had a full Meissen china tea set for example.

For her good humour, ready wit and infectious laughter, Morgana was known by most people as the Merry Widow and was an immensely popular figure in the area. Shortly after her seventieth birthday however, her friends noticed a slight failing in her memory. The occasional missed appointment or a repeated piece of conversation started to ring warning bells. Mr Young senior was one of those who picked it up early and was close enough to Morgana to mention it. As a joke at first, but as things progressed he felt obliged as both a friend and legal adviser to formally suggest that Morgana sought medical advice about the possibility of having Alzheimer's disease or something of that nature. Morgana was initially insulted, but as she saw the tender look of concern in her friend's eyes she reluctantly agreed and made an appointment with her GP, her first for many years.

After a second appointment with a specialist and a wide range of tests Morgana's GP had to break the news to her that she had the early stages of dementia and it was likely to get progressively worse. Mr Young senior had been invited along and Morgana was pleased he had accepted the invite. She was aware of becoming more forgetful but then, wasn't that part and parcel of old age? The diagnosis confirmed that it was far more than that and she needed someone about whom she could trust implicitly with her future welfare. After the appointment with the GP the two friends headed for the lawyer's office for a serious planning meeting.

"Well it's not just the usual problems of old age is it?" Morgana began.

"I'm afraid not, old girl. It's more serious and it's progressive."

"Okay then, we need to plan ahead for the time that I am completely gaga and can't make my own decisions. You'll have to do it all for me, George."

"That is of course possible. It would be better to involve at least one family member as early as possible, to ensure there are no allegations of conflict of interest. It would also be advisable to have an independent solicitor involved in the drawing up of any power of attorney document. That will require you to behave normally for about an hour or so. You've never really done that in your life but there is a first time for everything."

They laughed briefly before agreeing that George would arrange the legal side of things and Morgana would contact her relatives, no matter how distant, and find one who was willing to help her. They kissed each other on the cheek, perhaps a little more fondly than usual, and then separated to focus on their individual parts of the plan.

As an only child, Morgana had no siblings and therefore no nieces or nephews with blood ties. Her late husband, however, had a brother and a sister, both of whom had children. Dr Robertson's siblings had grown up in the old manse, and during the early years after it became the oldest brother's home they had been frequent visitors. This had continued as each married, and their own offspring had enjoyed the space of the Manse and the surrounding countryside on visits during the long school holidays. As Morgana's three nieces and two nephews grew older they went their own ways and eventually stopped visiting all together. Morgana's brother and sister-in-law had also stopped visiting on a regular basis after Dr Robertson died and contact had dwindled to the obligatory Christmas cards and a dutiful phone call each New Year and again on Morgana's birthday. As her birthday was in February, the bulk of the year passed with largely no contact between the three. There was no enmity and there had been no falling out; they had simply had little in common beyond the ties created by marriage.

Morgana found herself struggling to know how to raise the matter with the members of her late husband's extended family. She wasn't going to phone and ask for help. Not yet anyway. It was more a notification process that had to be gone through. She knew they would be sympathetic but she did not want any fuss. Not now or even later. They had to be informed, and one of them would be invited to have power of attorney along with George. Beyond that, nothing had to be done for, she hoped, some time. They would, after all, be the beneficiaries of her estate after generous provision for a range of Morgana's charities and close friends. She did not know how much would be involved but was shrewd enough to realise that it would be well worth her brother's family attending the reading of the will.

'No time like the present' had been her motto for any duties good or bad, and there was no reason to put things off. After making herself a cup of coffee she sat down on the uncomfortable chair next to the house phone and called first her brother-in-law. Fortunately he was in at the time and after initial surprise at the call he realised the importance of it and was immediately sympathetic. Morgana hadn't to worry about a thing. He and Ruth would handle everything when the time came and Morgana could stay with them when she was no longer able to look after herself. Assuring him that that was a long with off, she thanked him and asked him to let his children know too.

The next call was to her sister-in-law who, as usual, was out. Her husband was in but Morgana preferred to deliver the news to her sister-in-law personally. 'No, it was nothing important. If Susan could phone back sometime when it suited that would be fine.'

Morgana put the phone down and went into her kitchen to make a cup of coffee. 'Where was that cup of hers? She had had it just a moment or so ago.' Meanwhile the untouched cup of coffee grew cold next to the phone; the first of many to be made and then forgotten about.

Morgana's sister did phone back but by then had heard the news from her brother. She too was all sympathy and reassured Morgana that they would both rally round and help in any way they could. The nieces and nephews had all been informed too and a support network would be in place for Morgana from that moment on. The offer of help seemed to be genuine and Morgana relaxed. With George at the helm and family on call perhaps she could manage the effects of the illness with dignity.

Amongst the nieces and nephews however, the news had had mixed effects. The two nephews were busy people and had children of their own. Two of the nieces were also married and had families. These four had agreed to help if they could, but had secretly doubted it would ever be necessary. Only the remaining unmarried niece, Isobel Robertson, had shown immediate interest. She had not been gifted with looks or good luck and resented the success and popularity of her brother and sister. She had struggled through school and afterwards had flitted from one dead end job to another over the years, returning home to mum and dad on a regular basis when out of funds. There was nothing wrong with her memory though, in particular her memory of dear Aunt Morgana's treasure house in the Scottish Borders.

When she heard that her poor old aunt was suffering from dementia, and being between jobs herself at the time, she offered to visit the Old Manse and to assess what help Morgana might need. She might even stay for a while or move in and help as her aunt's memory failed. Especially as her memory of what antiques were in the house started to falter. Lawyers often say, where there's a will, there's a relative. In some cases where there's a will there's a relative unwilling to wait for the minor detail of the benefactor's demise.

So it was with Isobel. She headed for her aunt's house like a guided missile and after oozing sympathy for her plight took up permanent residence in the Old Manse. Some of the villagers vaguely remembered her from her childhood visits, others mistook her for Morgana's daughter. Either way it was universally acknowledged that Isobel had been a godsend to the Merry Widow and could not do enough for her from day one. Shopping, laundry and household chores were done and everything which Morgana had been in the habit of doing was written out on a huge planner which appeared in the kitchen. Morgana had been advised to stop driving by then as she had forgotten her way home on at least two occasions, so Isobel took on the role of chauffeuse, using Morgana's car of course. This arrangement initially put Morgana's friends' minds at ease. Here was a relative prepared to move in and selflessly look after her failing aunt. Morgana could relax as could her friend and advisor George Young senior, who had wisely arranged for both Morgana's brother-in-law and sister-in-law to be given power of attorney along with himself, thus ensuring that everyone who might benefit from Morgana's estate in the future was fully involved in the decisions about her welfare while she was still alive. Everyone seemed happy with the new arrangement, especially Isobel, who began to make increasingly frequent visits to the antique shops and auction houses of Edinburgh and was often to be seen on her nights off with large bundles of cash in one of the two local hotels.

On one such visit to The Reiver she was spotted in the company of a surprisingly young and attractive male friend. As they got more and more intimate after a very long, expensive meal together, the watching crowd at the bar noticed that Isobel was paying for everything and she was pulling notes from a large wad of money in her handbag. The crowd were intrigued by this, none of them more so than Robbie Buchanan.

Chapter 23

The Rev and Mrs Sommerville

The church in Kirkton was the charge of the Rev William Sommerville who had recently entered the ministry following a highly successful career in retailing. His wife Rosemary had been a staunch churchgoer all her life and had married William for love and in spite of his lack of faith. She had tolerated this and his refusal to go to church during the early years of their marriage with patience and much clever banter. When their two sons were born, however, she stood her ground in a long and protracted discussion of whether the boys would be raised within the Christian faith. In the end she had won, or perhaps just worn William down, to the point that it had been agreed she would take the boys to church with her each Sunday. William was absolved from any such duties if she was ill or away for any reason. As a result the boys grew to look forward to their mother's trips to nurse their granny between her numerous operations. They loved their granny and wished her no harm but if she was ill anyway and Rosemary had to attend to her on a regular basis it was a definite positive that they would also miss church.

To William's dismay his youngest son became quite devout and started to insist on going to church even if his mother was away. In the end William found himself accompanying Daniel to the service for the sake of an easy life. To his surprise he found that the hour-long service was actually the only part of the week where he had the opportunity to relax. His thoughts were rarely centred round the Father, Son or indeed the Holy Ghost, but he did have time for thinking. His working day was so hectic, involving as it did the management of a medium-sized supermarket for a national company that he had no other opportunity to be alone with his own thoughts.

As a result he started to almost look forward to Sunday 'church time' as he called it. He even went along with Rosemary and the boys on the occasions when his shift rota permitted. Looking back over the years he could not pinpoint the moment when his own thoughts were interrupted by the words of the Rev Douglas Souter. Douglas was an aging career minister in the Church of Scotland and although he had watched his parishes shrink over the years he was realistic enough to know that this was the pattern throughout the Church of Scotland and indeed the established churches of the UK as a whole. He could comfort himself in the thought that his parish had contracted less than others. His faith did not waiver, not even with the untimely death of his wife, Rachel, from cancer when they were both in their mid-fifties. "God calling the best to heaven early," he had said unselfishly. The years had seemed longer after that and he rarely saw any evidence of the Lord working through his ministry. He lived in hope, however, that he might inspire somebody younger to take up the baton with the vigour and energy he had once had. Even seeing fresh faces in the congregation from time to time would cheer him up immensely, especially if they were under retiral age.

It was therefore with great pleasure that he noticed the husband of one of his favourite parishioners had started to accompany the rest of his family. He knew Rosemary well from the Woman's Guild, as a Sunday School teacher, a Cub leader, a member of the kirk session and therefore one of the first woman elders in the parish. They had discussed William's lack of faith on many occasions and Mr Souter had urged patience each time with little expectation of a road-to-Damascus-type conversion in this case. The best he could hope for was a near-death-bed conversion for William, though that would almost certainly be long after he himself had joined his wife in God's house. William's attendance was therefore a pleasant surprise and he read more into it than he initially should have done. But he should have taken his own advice and been patient.

As William's attendance became a more regular feature and the pressures of retail in the fast lane started to take their toll, he found himself listening to the minister's words to see what all this peace and tranquillity his wife took for granted was about. Slowly but surely some of it hit home and he started to question his lifestyle. He earned a very good salary as a branch manager and was young for his grade. Noises had been made at his annual appraisals about him flying higher and getting a position in regional management. He had the right stuff etc. This had always made him feel good until now. The trade-off for all this had been long hours and missing a great part of his children growing up.'Sell your soul to the company and the company will look after you', he had always believed. If money and prestigious company car were the measures of success then he was doing well and the company was indeed looking after him and by extension, his family. But was that enough in exchange for his soul? The Rev Douglas Souter saw a more attentive face in the crowd as he preached and played to it with every bit of his ability and experience.

"It is easier for a camel to pass through the eye of a needle than for a rich man to enter the kingdom of

God." "What does it profit a man if he gains the world but loses his soul?"

All these and more seemed to strike a note with William as Rev Souter preached and the good reverend too began to believe: to believe that he could save a soul. Perhaps even find the younger man to whom he could pass on the baton.

It was Douglas' habit to stand at the door of the church after each service and to shake hands and pass a word or two to each of his parishioners as they left. This allowed him to achieve a number of things. He could gauge the impact of his sermon on the flock. Some members would look forward to telling him in no uncertain terms, good or bad. It gave him the opportunity to pass on praise or sympathy where appropriate. He could welcome new members or visitors to the church and village. Perhaps also it afforded an opportunity for a head count to make sure his flock were all still alive.

He began to take these opportunities to have a brief word with William. At first it was a casual "nice to see you again" or similar pleasantry. It soon began to be more lengthy chats and he noticed that William would deliberately hold back so that he could engage the minister in conversation without delaying any other members of the congregation. This developed into a tentative invite from Douglas for William and Rosemary to dine at the manse. This one occasion was such a success that Rosemary had returned home early and alone to relieve the baby-sitter, leaving the men to discuss faith and the pressure of working-life together for several hours afterwards.

When William had eventually left for home, oblivious of the passage of time during the discussions, Mr Souter took the unusual step of pouring himself a small whisky, heavily diluted with water. He switched the radio on and sat down in his favourite chair in front of an unlit fire. It was not a celebratory drink he assured himself, not yet, but he felt a feeling of hope for the church which had been rare of late. The mood lasted until the voice on the radio introduced "an old favourite"; one of Robert Burns finest love songs 'Ae Fond Kiss'. It was the one song guaranteed to remind Douglas Souter of the loss of his wife, but he left it on.

"Ae fond kiss and then we sever"

He found himself humming along.

"ae fareweel, and then for ever..."

He felt a tear form in his left eye and could not stop it. The record continued relentlessly.

"Dark despair around benights me.... "

The tear ran down his cheek as he finished his drink. He looked up and whispered: "You are a difficult master sometimes." Then he went to bed.

This one meal soon led to William regularly dining with Douglas after Sunday worship. Rosemary was delighted. In the words of one of her favourite contemporary apostles, Bob Dylan, it had been "a slow train coming", but William's conversion was now well under way. It was therefore a well-anticipated surprise when Douglas announced with pleasure that one of the congregation had received a calling and was about to embark on his training for the ministry. There was a polite gasp of false surprise from the aging flock when William's name was mentioned. Rosemary sat beside him with a proud smile on her face and nodded to friends as William was invited to read the day's lesson; Luke 15:4 and Psalms 119:176. There were knowing smiles and glances between William and the congregation as he read about lost sheep. He had never felt surer of himself as he did that day, reading the Bible in his church, ready to become a minister of God.

His studies went well and in due course he was ordained and given the small and rural charge of Kirkton ("for my sins", he would joke). He moved to the manse there with his wife and children excited about their new life. The children had been less excited at first but, with William having taken voluntary redundancy and sold their large family home, the Sommervilles had been able to put a large amount of money away and indulged their children as a bribe to ease the stress of moving. This seemed to do the trick, and William and Rosemary were able to look forward to his first service as the new minister with relatively no dissenting voices in the manse. The Rev Douglas Souter had arranged cover for his own church specially in order to attend and sat in the front row, beaming from ear to ear. The service was relatively well attended and extremely well received. William had put a huge effort into his maiden sermon in his first charge, using a lot of witty references to shopping and loyalty points along the way. Tea and coffee flowed afterwards and the whole village seemed to be looking forward to a new era of ministry with the bonus for the local school of a young family in the manse.

As afternoon wound on, Douglas took leave of his young protégé , whispering in his ear, "Good Luck William. May you find the riches you have been seeking in your work here." Then he made his way to his car and drove home. He had enjoyed the day immensely and was very proud of William's powerful preaching style. Despite this, though he felt a weight in his heart that he could not easily explain. Once home he made a light supper and again poured himself a whisky diluted with water and sat in his favourite chair. He put on the digital radio using the remote, a thank you present from William and Rosemary. He ate slowly and sipped at the whisky, enjoying the background music while he reflected on William's journey of faith. It had been an exciting and enjoyable time for both men and Douglas should have felt elated at the result, but again, instead there was a feeling of having a heaviness in his heart. The feeling increased until he realised that it was physical rather than an emotional state. The weight turned to a pain which spread to his left shoulder and arm. He tried to rise but could not. He put down the sandwich he had been holding and picked up his glass. Taking a sip despite the shaking in his right hand he tried to replace the glass on his table but now could not.

On the radio a voice introduced the next song, the unmistakable Robert Burns love song, 'ae fond kiss'.

"ae fond kiss and then we sever:

Ae fareweel, and then forever!"

Douglas again tried to rise but was paralysed down his left side and sat motionless instead. A familiar tear formed in his eye and trickled down his cheek. He could no longer move to wipe it away. The singer continued mercilessly.

"Who shall say that Fortune grieves him,

While the star of hope she leaves him?"

Douglas felt his mouth tremble on the left hand side and his leg spasm too. He was weakening by the second and the whisky glass fell from his hand, smashing on the floor. He heard it but could do nothing about it. "Somebody else's job now," he thought to himself. "Everything was somebody else's job now." The singer sang on, twisting the emotions of a helpless Douglas as he went.

"ae fond kiss and then we sever!

ae fareweel, alas, for ever!"

As the song finished, the Rev Douglas Souter passed away to meet his maker, his work finished and, all being well, to be reunited with his beloved wife Rachel.

Chapter 24

Saving Jennifer's Bottom

Jennifer Allerdyce was in a jam. Asking for millions of dollars and pounds from the Americans once was bad enough. Having to ask them for the money again because the first lot had gone missing was too much. At least, it was too much to expect without having something substantial to give in return and that meant she needed the passports and driving licences Brad had requested for the president before she could approach him for replacement funds. This she had eventually achieved after a very uncomfortable interview with her boss Sir Alan Sherbrooke, who almost certainly would be the next head of MI6. She could feel her chances of replacing him in due course evaporating as the meeting progressed.

"How had that amount of money slipped out of our hands? Who was the pilot? How had he been selected? Why had he given the two Americans a lift? Who had authorised that? What pressure had been brought to bear by the CIA for them to be transported too? Hadn't there been tracking devices in place? How quickly had the cases been located? How thoroughly had the HGV driver Roberton been checked out? What efforts were now in place to recover the funds?"

Sir Alan's questioning went on in a forensic manner, covering every aspect of the whole sorry affair. Jennifer had prepared for the meeting thoroughly and was able to answer the questions, in specific detail, each time. As he continued though, with question after question she felt that he must be thinking seriously about her future. Every question felt like a nail in the coffin of her career.

"Why did you select Robbie Buchanan? What is his cover story? Have you informed the Americans yet?"

On and bloody on he went till at last he stopped and paused. It seemed as if he had honestly asked every possible question he could. Jennifer was sure of it. She racked her brain for any little detail that had been left out. Sir Alan had a joint first from Cambridge in Mathematics and Classical Arabic. His IQ was in the top 0.001 of the population. He had acquired a PhD in his spare time along with separate degrees in History, Philosophy, Politics and Economics. An MBA had been added during a sabbatical year in the States. He had written four standard academic texts on Moorish history and culture. Had he chosen to include all the post nominal letters available to him on his business cards they would have needed to be on A4 paper to be legible. Despite all this, he was also pretty street smart.

After a pause he looked at Jennifer with a relaxed expression. "You appear to have done everything possible in this case to achieve the necessary task. Now how do we get the Americans to replace the money?"

Jennifer tried to stifle the sigh of relief as he said this and ended up swallowing and burping simultaneously. But she was ready with the answer.

"They will cough up again if their President can get these passports and driving licences."

She handed the list to Sir Alan who raised a largely unexercised eyebrow.

"Really," he said. "Do we know what they will be used for?"

"No details given or likely to be," Jennifer answered.

"Are you sure the request is from the President? Don't they realise we will be monitoring their every use? Can we get assurances they won't be used against European powers?"

'Shit,' thought Jennifer, 'he's off again'.

After a second detailed interrogation, Sir Alan had given Jennifer the necessary authority to get the documents

Brad had asked for. Her relief was palpable but tempered by the fact that she now had to meet Brad again and ask him for more money. Yes, the documents would make that far easier but she knew she would have to suffer his feigned shock and his gratuitous drivelling on about how he would have to pull strings to save her butt.

The meeting between Brad and Jennifer went very much as she had predicted. He had been shocked at the loss of two US agents. Shocked to find out that not only had the money gone missing but that neither MI6 nor MI5 had managed to trace it to date. The documents were all very well but this was a lot of money. Maybe he could save her ass. Maybe he could avoid her getting spanked in public. His ass was on the line too. He went on and on. In all, Jennifer counted twenty nine references to her backside and four to Brad's own. He was obsessed, but eventually, as he reached the end of the pantomime he agreed to replace the funds. Also he wanted Jennifer to keep looking for the missing money as a matter of priority and to hand it over to him when they found it. This time though he would arrange for the funds to be delivered directly to the training camp where the Syrian rebels were being trained by American assets.

"Don't want another Brit pilot who doesn't know his ass from his elbow."

"A third person's bottom," Jennifer groaned inwardly. She had decided to take a shower and change her underwear after the meeting was finished. Inexplicably, it somehow felt soiled now.

They parted as usual with a hand shake and nothing else. Jennifer knew this time the handshake was to seal a deal. Brad had got the documents his President wanted and Jennifer had replaced the missing money at nil cost to HM's Government. It was yet another trade of principle in the face of necessity.

"That was the bottom line," she thought to herself before groaning, "Oh don't you start."

With the immediate problem of replacing the money solved, Jennifer now had to decide what to do about the missing millions. Robbie had impressed her with his diligence and enthusiasm for the task thus far but at the end of the day he had produced nothing, certainly none of the cash. He had narrowed the list down to an extent but it all smelled of guess work to her. Brad had laboured the point that the Americans wanted their money back from the first consignment, and whether that was true or not she knew that he would hold it over her head as long as he could. She shivered involuntarily. That was the last thing she wanted as she positioned herself towards the top job and an appointment as Dame Jennifer Allerdyce, first female Chief of MI6.

The question, in a way, boiled down to how urgent she regarded the problem as being. If she wanted a quick resolution she would have to allocate scarce resources to assist or replace Robbie. If it was important but not urgent she could allow him to continue on his own with support from London at relatively little cost in money or personnel. Allocating troops to the task would highlight to anyone interested that a large sum of money had gone missing on her watch. She wasn't keen on that option for a whole host of reasons. Patience might be the best approach here. Softly, softly, catchy monkey and all that. Robbie might take a while but she was confident he would find the money eventually. After all, as far as he was concerned his salary depended on it. Once traced, she could task a couple of members of the increment to recover it and then shove it down Brad Dexter's throat, if only to shut him up. Sadly it would only be metaphorically. She decided to phone Robbie.

"Mr Buchanan, how are you getting along?" she inquired. "Or to cut to the chase, have you found any of our colonial cousins' missing money yet?"

"As you well know from my regular conversations with my link in London, no, not yet. However, I am making progress with the list of suspects, which is narrowing nicely. I need some more time to whittle it down further, or for somebody to slip up and show their hand."

"Time is not something I have to play with," lied Jennifer. "I expect you to be able to point out two or at the most three likely contenders by the end of next week. Is that crystal clear? I wouldn't like to be paying somebody a salary for nothing. That would be very hard to justify to my superiors."

"No offence, but how come my pay is under review at exactly the same time as you need someone to do a bit of undercover work for you without anybody knowing about it?"

"It is one of life's many strange coincidences. Whatever the timing of it I do have your file here and it does seem difficult to justify the expenditure of your salary without getting something in return. I suggest you make full use of your time there over the next week before we talk again. Obviously an earlier phone call to inform me of success would be preferable for all concerned. Good bye and good luck, Mr Buchanan."

With that Jennifer put the phone down and smiled. She was enjoying this little game now. She would enjoy it even more if she could tell Brad where his money was, even if she couldn't tell him where to put it, tempting as that might be.

Chapter 25

Brad Flies a Kite

Brad headed back to the US embassy in high spirits. Not only had he saved Jennifer's ass yet again, a favour she had to repay one way or another, but he had got her assurance that Brad would be able to deliver the President's requested documents. That would be a huge feather in his cap. It had sounded a non-starter when the commander in chief had spoken to Brad on the phone. Although he had assured the President at the time that he would do everything he could to secure the documents, he had little confidence he could deliver. Under Tony Blair it seemed that anyone making a home run to Britain got a UK passport as a prize, but things had changed since then. They were also a bit tight with anyone who wasn't actually in the country already. Now, though, he could phone back the chief of staff at the White House no less and say 'job done'. Brad Dexter of the CIA had got them from the Brits. No problem. No sweat. He could see a medal of some kind heading his way for that one, not to mention his choice of promoted posts. Oh yes. It had been a good day alright.

The next thing to do was to keep the pressure up on Jenny baby till she cracked. He could picture her having to agree to a liaison with him; a rendezvous in an expensive hotel or a safe house, just to save her career. Oh yes, he had her ass over a barrel. All he had to do was make sure she never got her hands on the missing money. It was chicken feed in the big picture of things, and he suspected the President would authorise far more to obtain the Brit passports and driving licences, given the way he had spoken to Brad. But Jennifer need not know that and neither did her superiors. No, if he got to the missing money first without her knowledge and kept up the pressure on her then she would be right where he wanted her to be. What he needed now was someone to find the money before MI5 or MI6 did and he knew just who to ask: his old friend Jonathan 'the bag man' Cusack.

Jonathan Cusack had been a CIA employee forever. He could talk about missions in places which most CIA field agents had never had to study on a map. He had travelled the world moving people, equipment and cash for 'the firm'. His knowledge of the logistics of clandestine warfare was second-to-none, and he had stretched the use of the term 'diplomatic bag' beyond recognition. Everything from handguns to a Jumbo Jet had been exported when necessary using that archaic phrase; hence his nickname of 'the bag man'. He not only knew field agents in every corner of the globe but he also knew a wide range of freelance operators who could be employed at very short notice to carry out jobs which the agency needed to be able to deny any connection with, if necessary. Often these people were referred to as 'kites'; any problems and their connection was cut allowing them to fly away freely and creating plausible deniability. Brad had used Jonathon's services on several occasions, including while based in London and knew that he would know suitable kites to track down the missing money.

"Jonathan, how are they hanging?" asked Brad when he reached Jonathan by secure phone.

"About right, my friend," came the standard reply. "I assume you're my friend at the moment if you are phoning me for a favour."

"Au contraire, mon amigo, I am phoning to do you a favour," countered Brad.

"That sounds as unlikely as it sounds worrying."

"I swear. Would I lie to you?"

"Yes and you have done on numerous occasions. However I am willing to suspend my disbelief again for old time's sake. What favour are you going to do for me?"

"I know where about six million dollars of cash went missing, some of it in sterling, and I want to give it to you on plate."

"Somehow I feel there must be more to it than that. Am I right?" asked Jonathan.

"No, honestly, this money is missing in a tranquil, gun-free friendly state and has already been officially and unofficially written off. All I want you to do is select some deserving souls from your address book and make sure they find it before MI6. They find it: they get to keep it. Simple as that. You can agree a split with them if you wish. This is a strictly don't-need-to-know mission on my part. What do you say, buddy?"

"I assume we are talking somewhere particularly dangerous here?" asked Jonathan, confused.

"No, here's the sweetest part. It's in the Scottish Borders."

Jonathan knew how to safely cross the most dangerous borders in the world and had done so on many, deniable occasions but this border was a new one on him.

"Where?"

"The Scottish Borders, in England. Hills, valleys, whisky and nothing else really. A piece of cake. I need two of your best there by tomorrow. I mean it when I say they get to keep the money. The details are on their way to you now."

"Okay Brad, if you say so. What about the competition?"

"Nothing to worry about at all. The police don't know about it and the Brits are playing it really low key. My source says they only have one guy on it; a cripple they sacked years ago just sniffing about in the dark. He's unarmed as well as missing a leg," Brad sniggered at his own wit. "The police don't even carry guns there. Anyway, tell me when it's done."

"Sure thing, buddy. By the way you do realise it is strictly forbidden for any agency employee to accept payment from any source outwith official remuneration?"

"Yeh, so I'd heard," replied Brad and hung up.

Jonathan opened the email which had arrived on his PC in Langley from Brad. He read through the details and chuckled. He also looked up the village of Kirkton on Google maps and chuckled again. On the face of it this was the easiest and safest task he had been handed in years. All he needed were two freelancers in the UK at the moment who fancied six million dollars' worth of cash for a few days' work. How difficult could that be? Brad's suggestion of a cut for himself had been a joke, he assumed. It was, of course, strictly against the rules to pocket any cash except your salary although everything he did most days was against somebody's rules. The CIA's rules were different though. They were binding in a far stronger way than the law of the land. He had two years to go before retirement and wasn't about to mess it up now. He could actually have retired a year ago but was asked to stay on and did, fearful he would get bored away from the agency and it was a fixed term extension to his career.

He checked his files and current locations notes and saw just the two charmers he needed for this job; Steve Huizman and Lance Shultz. Two of the finest reprobates he had ever employed. They had been Special Forces, SEALs to be specific and had fallen foul of official discipline there. The agency was always on the lookout for their type when they left the military by whichever route, and had employed them from time to time. In between unofficial work for the CIA, they had worked in Iraq and Afghanistan as private security guards. His file suggested other, more criminal activities around the world too, but nothing he had seen said US territory on it so they were fine by him. They appeared to be kicking their heels on a low-paid job in London for the Israelis at the moment and he knew they would jump at the chance of this kind of payday. After a quick phone call, Steve and Lance were on their way to the Scottish Borders in a rented people-carrier, to do a bit of fishing.

God help the poor people of Kirkton, mused Jonathan. They don't know what's about to hit town.

Chapter 26

American Fishermen

Weather-wise, the day had started badly and fallen away since. A thin drizzle as most people woke up had developed into heavy rain which showed no inclination to stop anytime soon. In fact, if anything, the rain was getting heavier as the long day wore on. The retired population was largely staying indoors, except to walk dogs quickly and return to the fireside and dry clothes. The farmers were out working as ever, but beyond the essential tending of livestock even many of them were heading for an early bath. By six o'clock in the evening nobody was milling about outside if they had any sense. In Kirkton, that limited the number to about four or five. When the thunder and lightning arrived it convinced the undecided to go indoors and stay there. For many, 'indoors' included the option of one of the two pubs. As the thunder and heavier rain rolled in at one end of town, a large dark people-carrier rolled in at the other. Its dark threatening presence was noted by everyone who was drinking at the Reiver Hotel.

On this particularly unpleasant evening, Robbie had decided to have a few pints in the Reiver Hotel in Little Kirkton. He sat amongst a now familiar group of locals, which included George and the lady with dyed red hair, whose name was Maggie, sitting in a corner with yet another new man. When she left with him after a drink, Robbie asked the barman who Maggie was with today with a wink. The barman looked at him as if to say "who do you expect?" before saying "her husband Bill, of course".

As a result he was there to witness the arrival of Lance and Steve, America's least likely salmon fishermen. They drove into the car park in a jet black Grand Voyager which matched the weather and their facial expressions perfectly. As they got out of the vehicle they looked more like heavyweight boxers rather than fishermen. If they had been, and this was the venue for the fight, they would have both turned round and gone home.

Walking into the public bar they forced smiles at the locals and visitors sheltering from the storm and stated the obvious. "Hell of an evening."

"Aye," agreed George on behalf of the local group.

"Any rooms tonight?" asked Lance.

Young Robbie the Pub was on duty that night and as ever had no idea whether the hotel was full, empty or closed for refurbishment.

"I'll check for you," he replied with his customary cheerfulness and headed off to the office.

Lance and Steve ran a forensic eye over the assembled crowd in the bar. Most were clearly retirement age. One looked like it but probably wasn't. A tough life of heavy drinking was writ large on the lines around his eyes and his skin tone. Two were most likely walkers visiting the village, going by the steam coming off their clothes and boots as they thawed themselves out beside the fire. Besides the barman, that left a middle aged lady, who may or not be accompanying any of the other men and the younger man at the far end of the bar. Lance recognised in him the lean look of a soldier or similar and this impression was reinforced by the thousand yard stare he had fixed on Lance and Steve. Robbie smiled back and turned back to continue the conversation he had been trying to avoid having with George.

Robbie the Pub returned and confirmed that there was a twin room available for up to three nights if they wanted it. Steve confirmed they would take it for the full three days without asking the price. He offered to bring in the luggage if Robbie the Pub would show him the room and if Lance would get the beers in.

Lance looked round at the beer taps and recognised nothing." What are you guys drinking?" he asked, before realising his mistake.

"That's very kind of you," said George, "I'll have a pint of lager."

Others joined in and Lance was forced to buy six drinks or look stupid. He tried a smile but it was more worrying than reassuring to the company at the bar, so he returned to his usual expressionless self. He noticed that the man at the end of the bar had not asked for a drink and was still looking him up and down as if to take in every aspect of his person – which, of course, Robbie was.

"Are you here to fish?" asked George who had noticed the compartmented fishing waistcoats which both Lance and Steve were wearing.

"That's right," said Lance, "We hear you guys have the best salmon fishing in the world."

Callum the ghillie looked up from his Guinness with professional interest and engaged Lance in conversation about salmon fishing on the nearby river Tweed where he worked. After five minutes though, he realised that Lance knew nothing about salmon fishing and gave up. This exchange intrigued Robbie whose suspicions had been aroused when the Americans had arrived. Callum could talk for hours about catching just one fish, and days if fuelled by whisky. If he had given up on an apparent opportunity like this so quickly then this American was no fisherman of salmon or anything else for that matter.

"Interesting," he thought to himself.

Steve returned and gave Lance a signal with his left hand which probably indicated the rooms were okay. It might have meant that there were no electronic bugs in the room: or any kind of bugs. Perhaps it meant they were masons; whatever it signified it wasn't noticed by any of the locals aside from Robbie. Steve ordered Bourbon with ice and pointedly didn't buy a drink for anyone else.

He looked round and immediately clocked Robbie as the odd man out. He didn't look like a prosperous local who might have recently found a few million of mixed currencies. He might be someone else on the trail of it though and any rival for that kind of money was expendable by definition. He smiled at Robbie who smiled back, completely unfazed.

The evening followed the usual pattern, with most of the locals leaving to go home for a meal while diners arrived to eat at the Reiver. Robbie left early, deciding not to engage in conversation with the two Americans he thought were probably there on an identical mission to himself. Callum the ghillie left shortly before and the others soon afterwards. By seven thirty, only George was left in the bar, hoping for more free drink.

Lance and Steve had arrived with no clear plan beyond settling into Kirkton under the cover of being fishermen and tapping into anyone prepared to sell information for hard cash, English pounds if necessary. They had all the information the CIA could give them which was essentially what MI5 and MI6 had gathered before they realised the CIA were sending a team to carry out the same task as Robbie. Beyond that, Langley had come up with little of use beyond a large expenses budget. As a result they had arrived keen to find someone local who could give them the lowdown on the entire village of Kirkton and its inhabitants. As the crowd at the bar of the Reiver thinned and only George, Lance and Steve were left, it appeared that Karma was an American that night.

Steve looked at George and asked the opener, "You lived here long?"

"All my days really. Apart from when I lived in North Shields, of course."

The two Americans studied him for any sign of humour and found none.

"So you'll know everyone who lives here, then," chipped in Lance.

"Oh yes, everything," confirmed George.

"Everyone," corrected Steve.

"Everything about everyone," clarified George.

Steve and Lance exchanged a look which suggested they had hit pay dirt.

"You must have seen it all then," ventured Steve.

"By the way, what are you drinking... sorry I didn't catch your name," Lance encouraged.

"Macallan," answered George.

There was a pause before Robbie the Pub saved the day involuntarily by asking, "Is that a double Macallan, George?"

George didn't even check for confirmation from his benefactors before confirming that a double was fine, maybe with a half pint of real ale to wash it down.

Steve and Lance didn't flinch at George's generosity with their money. It was small beer, no pun intended. They had found a local they could pump for information and if the only cost was a few drinks they were on a roll.

"Oh I've seen it all in this valley," continued George. "Did you know aliens use the valley for refuelling?"

It was a worrying revelation to Lance and Steve.

They brought him back on track straight away.

"What about the folk here," asked Steve. "There must be some real stories to tell there?"

"Oh yes, I've seen them all come and go. The rich, the poor, the famous and the unknown."

This was better.

"A few folk got rich here then?" asked Lance.

"Oh yes," confirmed George.

"Anyone got rich here recently then? Steve and I are still looking to make our fortunes," probed Lance with a forced laugh.

"Oh yes," continued George. "Plenty of folk come in here with wads of cash. Some buy you drinks: Some don't. But you always know who just got rich."

"Yeh? Who's been flashing the cash here recently then?" asked Lance.

"Oh, not many recently. Just five or six."

Lance and Steve leaned forward on their respective barstools, encouraged by the low number suggested by their new inside source.

"Tell us more," suggested Lance, indicating to Robbie the Pub that the bottle of The MacCallan was handed to him and should be billed to the Americans' room.

"That bastard Barry the gamekeeper came in just last week with a wad of cash the size of my fist and bought drinks for all the beaters who work for him. Nothing for me, mind you."

"Sounds like he ain't your favourite person. What does he look like?" ventured Lance.

"Big heavy set bastard," continued George. "Always lines up the beermats and glasses till they are in a straight line. He has that OCDC thing. Walrus moustache and arms like a wrestler's thighs. Good dancer right enough."

Lance and Steve looked at each other and nodded. That was one possible on their list.

"There are that nice couple from the caravan site too. Walter and Bobby thingamajig. They always buy me a pint but won't take one back. They live in the Dolls House."

"They live in a doll's house at the caravan site?" queried Steve.

"No, no. They had a caravan and bought the Doll's House when it came up for sale. Sold their caravan. They didn't need it anymore did they?"

"The Doll's House?"

"Of course, next to the village shop."

"Two guys? Bobby and Walter? Not that I'm saying there's anything wrong with that," probed Steve, who felt there was something very wrong with that.

"Roberta's a good looking woman, not a bloke. Bobby for short."

Another nod was exchanged between the two Americans.

Robbie the Pub came through and handed the Americans two menus. He detailed the day's specials and asked if they preferred to eat in the bar or the dining room. Neither wanted their new-found source of intelligence to escape so they confirmed they would be happy to eat at the bar.

At that point Billy MacPherson came into the Reiver and ordered a cup of tea. He nodded at the Americans and briefly at George. On the basis of "it takes one to know one", he immediately recognised the Americans as ex-forces of some kind or another and engaged them in conversation. They recognised the same in him too and spoke on vaguely equal terms.

Robbie loitered in the background to take a food order.

"So what were you in, like," asked Billy.

"We were both SEALS," said Steve with pride.

"Have the fish," said George.

Steve spun round ready for a fight. He had heard every joke there was about the US Navy's Sea Air and Land Teams, the principle Special Operations Force of the US navy, and had started and finished a few fights to make the point that they took shit from nobody. He found George staring at a copy of the menu, oblivious to all around him.

"The breaded Eyemouth haddock. They serve the best there is here."

Steve forced himself to relax. "Sure, I'll give it a go," and he handed the menu back to Robbie.

"I'll have the venison burger," added Lance who wasn't exactly sure what that would be but figured a burger was a burger.

Billy made small talk for a while then left leaving Steve and Lance to finish their interrogation of George. For the cost of only a few more rounds they ended up with a list of five locals George confirmed had recently come into money:

Barry the gamekeeper, Mr and Mrs Crawley from Croydon who had retired a month ago to The Doll's House beside the village shop, the new minister and his wife and two locals called David and Clive who, according to George, were clearing mines from the valley for the government. There was mention of the Merry Widow's daughter but George was hazy on her name. To be honest, by that stage of the evening he was just hazy.

Steve and Lance thanked their new friend and waved him good bye as he headed unsteadily for his car, a blue Vectra with a dent in the back, with the remnants of the bottle of Macallan in his jacket pocket. Then they sat down to discuss the information they had acquired. It would be good to corroborate some of it at least but a quick search of each of the houses was sounding like a good way to proceed. George may have his faults, they realised, but he had fingered these people as having large amounts of cash in hand recently and the barman had nodded each time.

Having agreed an outline plan they tucked into the meal which arrived in front of them. The fish was tasty but not quite what Steve had expected. Lance had to admit the venison burger was one of the best burgers he had ever eaten. Washed down with a couple of pints of the local real ale, they retired to their room in a relaxed state, confident their fortunes were about to be made.

Chapter 27

Donna and the Americans

Lance and Steve realised after their first night that the two hotels gave them a good chance of hearing gossip from the village, especially if they found another person as willing to talk after a few drinks as George had been. For this reason they decided to alternate their time between the Reiver and the Wagon, trawling for information. They found themselves in the Wagon late in the afternoon of their second day in Kirkton chatting to a few locals and staring at Donna's breasts. Again they were caught out by her look/don't look approach to their display but it was clear to all concerned that she found the two hunky Americans of considerable interest and was flirting far more than usual.

Shortly after they had finished their meal, a large man entered the bar, dressed in camouflage patterned jacket and trousers. He walked up to the bar and started straightening the bar covers and beer mats till they were in a perfect line. Donna brought him a pint of beer without him having to ask for it and placed it down in front of him in an angry gesture, suggesting his arrival hadn't made her night. From the tidy bar counter Steve and Lance knew they had just met Barry the gamekeeper.

The two Americans left the table they had been sitting at for their meal and went over to the bar in order to get a better view of both Barry and Donna, for very different reasons. Steve was the same height as Barry while Lance was an inch or so shorter. They smiled at Barry as they reached the bar and then the two ends of the room eyed up the other end like boxers before a fight. Donna watched from the other side of the bar, keen to see what would happen. Barry turned away first and straightened the beer mats on the counter, unnecessarily. Lance and Steve looked at each other as if to say, there will be no trouble tonight, then they returned to the evening's task of chatting up Donna.

She was loving the attention but was enjoying Barry's discomfort even more. Most people would have drunk up and left by now with Barry trying to scare them off. It looked to Donna as if the fit and muscly Americans didn't do intimidated. It also looked like Barry would come off a very poor second if he tried anything with them. The more she thought about that the more it sounded like the icing on the cake for an exciting evening; Barry gets hospitalised before she ends up in bed with one of the yanks. Bring it on.

Having had the thought, she decided that it wouldn't take much to bring things to a head. She knew Barry's temper and short fuse would find it impossible to stand her flirting with anyone. Flirting with two guys who weren't scared of him would drive Barry mad. The tension in the air was tangible and she was about to crank it up a notch or two further.

"I gather you two are fishermen. What are you hoping to catch?" she began.

"Oh, anything we can get our hands on, the bigger the better," said Lance and winked at Donna.

"There are some beauties in this area," she replied winking back.

"So I see," said Lance.

The conversation continued in this vain with the innuendos becoming more and more crude and Barry becoming angrier and angrier. As Lance leered at Donna over the counter, Steve stared at Barry and watched him grow red. Steve wasn't sure what the deal was between these two locals but he figured he didn't much care. If Lance scored with the barmaid and this guy had a problem with it Steve was happy enough to sort him out.

It might be the only fun he got that night, after all. The more Steve stared at Barry and smiled at his discomfort, the more it looked as if Barry would snap and start a fight.

"Want a drink, buddy?" Steve asked Barry making it sound more of a challenge than an invitation.

"No," came the simple reply.

"What do you do for a living, dressed like that?" continued Steve pursuing one of his favourite hobby horses. He hated civilians wearing camouflage kit and pretending to be soldiers, especially if they were over-weight.

"Shoot things," hissed Barry in reply.

"You and me both. It's a small world."

Steve continued with his baiting of the gamekeeper, having great fun as he did it.

For Barry's part, he was seething. He watched the slightly smaller man stare at Donna and make increasingly suggestive comments. It looked like Donna was falling for the appalling line in chat and would probably sleep with him if Barry couldn't put a stop to it. The other guy was enjoying every moment of the scene and looked as if he could beat Barry in a fight with one arm behind his back. If that happened, Donna would laugh in his face every time she saw him from that moment on. He didn't think he could face that possibility. On the other hand, he didn't want to just do nothing and let this American have his wicked way with poor wee Donna. On balance he decided that discretion was the better form of valour and, giving the other three occupants of the bar a murderous look he walked slowly out of the Wagon. As he made it out to the car park he heard the unmistakable sound of laughter behind him and nearly went back inside.

"That your husband?" asked Steve in all seriousness.

"No, he's nothing, nothing at all to me. He used to live with my mother till she got sick of him and ran off. Now he acts like he's my dad but really he's just a dirty old pervert."

"You're much better off with a young pervert," quipped Lance.

"Or two," said Donna, winking at Steve. She had loved the way he had intimidated Barry. Somehow she found that a real turn-on. She knew Steve wasn't scared of Barry and was even surer that he could have beaten the shit out of him if it had come to a fight.

Outside Barry was fuming. Not only had Donna been lapping up the attention from the two Americans but he had also had to back down from a confrontation. He climbed into his pick-up truck and drove it down the main street, turning it round till it was under the faulty street light and hidden from view. There he waited, his mood festering like an open wound.

After what seemed like an age, the taller American came out of the hotel and climbed into the big black people carrier parked in the car park. So the wee guy is staying, thought Barry, trying to convince himself that he could take the other American in a fight. To his surprise though, Lance followed a few minutes later. So she had teased them and dumped them, laughed Barry to himself. Serves them right, he thought. Just as he was about to drive away, Donna appeared. She locked the front door of the hotel behind her and ran towards the American's vehicle, giggling like a schoolgirl. She jumped into the front and climbed over Lance till she was squashed between the two large men. Barry's blood pressure reached danger point again as Donna put an arm round each and kissed them both full on the lips. Barry reached round instinctively for his shotgun before remembering that he now left it at home when he went to the pub, on police advice. He had to admit, it was probably the only reason he was still out of prison.

The black people carrier drew away from the Wagon Hotel with Barry following behind. It headed towards the Reiver where all three occupants got out and walked over to the residents' entrance where Steve fumbled with a key to let them in. While he did so Donna jumped onto Lance's back and started slapping his bottom as if she was riding a horse. Steve got the door open and Lance galloped inside with Donna on his back. As he did so Steve raised her skirt and playfully slapped her backside over her knickers. Then the door slammed shut and Barry was left alone in the darkness of his pick-up.

"Somebody was going to pay for this evening's carry on," he promised himself, "and pay very dearly indeed."

Chapter 28

Lists of Suspects

In his bedroom in Betty's B&B, Robbie examined his short-list of suspects. He had reduced the list to 24 individuals or couples who could have discovered the missing millions. Against these he had annotated a set of initials which marked them as likely, possible or unlikely. Those who had been marked as likely, not only had been in the village at the time the money went missing but had since exhibited supporting actions to suggest they had excess cash in their possession or had something to hide. Asterisks against a few names indicated that they fell into all three categories. By this method he had reduced the list to eight 'likelies', three of which had asterisks against their names.

Both David and Clive the metal detectorists had asterisks against their names. Both had recently spent serious money on purchases and paid cash. Home improvements and new detectors had all been acquired, mainly with cash. They had also recently fallen out over something to do with a big find. They were both suspicious in their actions and suspicious of each other. Although nothing had been found in the search of Clive's house, Robbie felt he could not rule him out completely.

Barry the gamekeeper was as furtive a character as Robbie had ever met and paid for everything in cash, including his latest pick-up and the recently acquired Polaris all-terrain vehicle.

The Crawleys were anything but furtive, but seemed to have ready money available for anything they wished. Their large shed had been paid for in cash and they had both a new car and a new caravan in the driveway of their house.

The Sommervilles seemed very cash rich for clergy. As well as the small hatchback provided by the church for Walter to use when carrying out his duties they had a large and very new people-carrier in the driveway of the manse. From the registration, it had clearly been purchased after the money went missing. Neither the minister nor his wife, nor indeed either of their children, dressed like church mice and Robbie had noticed the kids had the latest gadgets, including one which had been released in a blaze of publicity the week before; one each, in fact, with all the available games to match.

Isobel Robertson had not been on the original list which had been sent through to Robbie but he had added her name based on her behaviour in the hotels of Kirkton and her habit of splashing cash. This in itself would not have been enough to place her firmly on the list but she was a very keen hill-walker and her duties looking after her aunt meant she was often to be seen walking late at night and in all weathers as she took her chances at escape. She had claimed within Robbie's hearing that she was trying to capture the spirit of her youth when she used to roam around the valley at all hours with her brother, sister and cousins, whatever the weather. This made her a strong contender in his eyes for someone who might have been out and about when the helicopter had got into difficulty. She was a big strong girl and had access to a car. She knew the surrounding area as well as anyone did who had actually grown up there.

Then there was the mystery benefactor in the village. Money had appeared for a number of local causes and appeals, always cash. It could easily be one of the other six suspects but Robbie had to work on the basis that it could be a seventh party until he could rule it out for sure.

Billy MacPherson was a reluctant likely. He showed no signs of having much cash at all. His main reason for remaining on the list was his likely movements on the evening in question. Indeed his likely movements any evening, whatever the question.

The question of how to go about pinning down the actual benefactor of the accident was his next problem. He could not follow all of these people every minute of every day on his own. Additionally, it had been made clear to him by Jennifer that the only resources available for the task would be the contact at the end of the phone in London and that even he had plenty of other things to do. Instead he would have to try to rule them in or out by trying to catch them red handed or track down the source of each suspect's ready cash.

Chapter 29

Lance and Steve Check Out

While Robbie sat in his bedroom in the Wagon Hotel, across the valley Steve and Lance sat in their room in the Reiver Hotel and looked at a remarkably similar list. The only difference was the absence of Billy MacPherson, whom they had ruled out almost by gut instinct alone. Admittedly they had been invited into his house for a cup of tea (which fortunately included the option of coffee) one afternoon whilst walking past. Old sailors together, they had shot the breeze about their experiences in the forces for almost two hours during which the Americans had seen no evidence of recent spending by Billy. There had been no hint in his conversation about finding cash or having cash or even what he would do if he did find cash. They had concluded that not only was he essentially uninterested in money but that he might also be the most straightforward and honest person they had ever met. If he had any bundle of cash available he hid it well. He was generous with what money he appeared to have but this was very limited, from what they had seen so far.

The rest of the list mirrored Robbie's, which was hardly surprising. Brad's contacts within MI6 had managed to keep him posted on the reports which Jennifer was getting, including the ever-shrinking list of suspects.

While Robbie thought through subtle ways of tracking down the funds, Steve and Lance wanted a quick resolution and a quick getaway from Kirkton thereafter with the money. Subtlety was not a word in their lexicon. Brad had insisted that they did not hurt anyone during their search for the missing cash, but beyond that there were no rules as such by which they had to abide. Their plan then was to carry out a search of each of the homes over the course of one 12 hour period, starting early one evening and continuing until they found the money. If that left a trail of destruction in their wake so be it. What they knew and Robbie did not, was that most of the notes had been sprayed with a radioactive isotope. Although it was low level and relatively harmless it could be detected with reasonable accuracy using the portable Geiger counter they had brought with them. They had also brought along a selection of the tricks of their trade, including passive night goggles and, through force of habit, a pistol each.

The key question to decide was the order of likelihood that each person on the list might have found the money. The other factor was a suitable order to raid the various houses to ensure that if the first break-in was discovered and reported to the police, Steve and Lance could continue to search the other houses without interruption. After detailed consideration, based on their training and the geography of the Rowent Valley they set out the order of attack.

First up was Isobel Robertson's house, or at least her aunt's. She seemed a very likely contender and the house was located on the edge of the village where they could enter and not be disturbed. Isobel herself had taken to eating in one of the hotels each night, leaving her aunt to dine alone.

If they struck a blank at the Old Manse they would then try the current manse. The Sommervilles had loads of spare cash from what they had seen and the house was on the opposite side of the village.

If neither of these houses produced the goods they would hit the Crawleys after the shop had finished its daily stock-check, then Clive and finally David within the village, in a straight line pattern rather than any likely order of possible guilt. If all else failed they would only have Barry's farmhouse to check out before leaving, and his house was well out of town on the way to the main road south. They hoped that it wouldn't be necessary to check all of the houses but if it was, this plan gave them the best chance of avoiding detection and making good their escape. They had decided to carry out their operation on the Tuesday after their arrival in the village, having successfully extended their stay at the Riever Hotel, as that night had the maximum number of clubs and social events on and therefore the best chance of searching the houses without disturbing the occupants.

When Tuesday arrived, Steve and Lance checked out of the Reiver Hotel, thanking the staff for a lovely stay and leaving a generous tip for them plus a few drinks in the barrel for George. The fact that they had never gone fishing or mentioned it much during their stay after the first night was ignored by all concerned. They packed their luggage into the large people- carrier and waved goodbye, before heading off towards the A68 and the supposed journey south. After 20 miles they stopped in a layby, tipped the seats back and tried to get some sleep before the night's activities.

At four o'clock the alarm on Steve's phone went off and the two men got out of the vehicle to stretch their legs and have a pee. The plan involved Steve driving round the properties in turn, dropping Lance off to carry out a search of each. For that reason Steve remained dressed in jeans and casual shirt while Lance changed into dark combat uniform and prepared the Geiger counter and passive night goggles for later when it got dark. If they had made up their list in the right order hopefully they could be long gone before nightfall, but as always, success lay in thorough preparation and planning. When Lance was ready they synchronised watches and Steve turned the people-carrier back towards Kirkton.

First of all he drove past the rear of the Old Manse with the side door facing the garden. Lance quietly slipped out of the vehicle and while he was still shielded from view by its bulk he pulled himself up and over the wall in one smooth, well-practiced motion. Steve drove on and by arrangement left the village and pulled into the first layby to the north. There he waited for a signal from his colleague.

Inside the garden, Lance moved swiftly towards the backdoor which, as they had anticipated was unlocked. He went quickly inside and listened for any sound of movement. Their observation had rightly judged that Isobel would be out of the house each Tuesday evening, having an early meal with one of her male friends. That left Morgana on her own but they had overheard Isobel reassure one of her men that she always slipped her aunt a sleeping pill and as a result she would be out for the count for the whole night. Lance took the Geiger counter from its pouch and switched it on. It was a very sensitive instrument and would detect any of the isotope on the cash easily if it had been moved around the house or was still stored there. He moved from room to room watching the needle on the screen as he went. There was not a hint of a reading. Not a single flicker of movement on the dial. He found the door of one of the upstairs bedrooms wide open and looked in cautiously. Inside an old lady was sound asleep on the bed. The room was in almost total darkness, screened by the thickest velvet curtains he had ever seen. That would be the elderly Aunt Morgana he thought. He traversed the room still checking the readings on the machine as he went. Despite his training and skill he was checking the screen so intently that he failed to see the old lady's handbag on the floor beside the bed. Tripping over it, he had to put his hand down on the bed to steady himself. The old lady stirred and looked up at him.

"Ah John, you're home at last," she said. "Come to bed and warm yourself through, you must be exhausted too."

She reached over and managed to grab a hold of Lance's wrist, gently but surprisingly firmly.

"Come to bed, John. They shouldn't call you out in the middle of the night unless it is absolutely necessary."

Lance tried to break free without hurting the old lady but she held him tightly.

"Get undressed and get into bed John. You've been gone so long I have missed you."

Lance realised that she was mistaking him for her husband the doctor, presumably forgetting in her growing confusion that he had been dead for over thirty years. He was reluctant to force himself free in case she fully woke up and screamed the house down. She might even have a push button alert system linked to her niece or the hospital. "It was ridiculous," he thought to himself. He weighed 220 pounds and could bench-press 300 in the gym and at this exact moment in time his plans were being thwarted by an old women who weighed seven stone wet. He didn't like the thought of her wet actually, as there was something of a smell emanating from underneath the covers. With a sudden flash of inspiration he leaned forward and whispered into her ear.

"I'll just go to the toilet then get my pyjamas on. You wait for me here sweetheart."

The old lady smiled and released his wrist.

"Don't be long John. I'll warm you up," she whispered as she turned over and went back to sleep.

That was close, thought Lance as he clicked the button on his radio three times in quick succession to let Steve know he had struck a blank at the first house. He left through the back door just as a voice upstairs starting calling again for John to come to bed.

"Let's hope that's not the best offer I get all night," he chuckled to himself as he cleared the wall and rolled into the open door of the people-carrier waiting for him on the other side, exactly where it had dropped him off. The vehicle sped away once he was safely inside.

"No luck, I take it?" enquired Steve from the front.

"Not the way you mean, no," replied Lance as they headed towards the current manse in Little Kirkton.

Once there, they followed the same pattern again and in two seconds, with the vehicle still moving, Lance had cleared the second wall of the evening and was inside the garden of Rev Sommervilles home. They knew that Mrs Sommerville would be at The Women's Rural till later in the evening and that she had dropped both the boys off at Judo on the way. They would be brought back later by another parent after the training session but that would not be for another two hours. That left Rev Sommerville, whose movements on Tuesday evenings were not known. Lance was ready for any eventuality, however, and was fully prepared to knock him out and tie him up if necessary. He and Steve had figured that would be within the spirit if not the letter of Brad's instructions.

This time Lance had to force the backdoor and winced as it creaked open. He slipped inside, ready for an inquisitive Rev Sommerville to appear. After five minutes he realised that nobody was coming. Perhaps this big house was so big that the minister had not heard the noise. Maybe he was praying so strongly that he had missed the loud noise from his back door. Lance continued through the large kitchen and into the hallway, checking the readings on the Geiger counter as he went. Again there was nothing indicated by the needle.

The door to the lounge was open and Lance could hear the sound of a television from inside. He also became aware of someone shouting abuse as if being beaten to within an inch of their life. There was foul language coming from the room which would have made a sailor blush and as an ex- US SEAL, Lance would know. Perhaps somebody had beaten him to it and was pounding the whereabouts of the money out of the minister. He moved quickly towards the room with a small cosh in his hand. Peeping inside he found the minister staring at the television screen with a helmet on his head and a game consul in his hand. Lance watched as the man of God slaughtered a series of soldiers in gratuitous 3D colour. The minister was wearing a set of head phones and, unaware of his observer, was shouting and swearing as he went. The carnage on the screen continued as Lance took a couple of readings from the doorway to confirm the room did not contain the missing cash. Then he quickly toured the house checking each room in turn.

As he headed towards the back door, again having failed to find a single trace of the money he heard a loud shout of, "You dirty little bastard!" coming from the front room. Not words the parishioners were likely to hear in a sermon, Lance judged. At the back door he again pressed the switch on his radio three times before retracing his steps and jumping back into the people-carrier.

He gave Steve the thumbs down sign and with a shrug Steve headed the vehicle towards the Doll's House where the Crawleys had recently set up home. The light was starting to fail as they reached the shop and Steve again slowed down so that Lance could sneak out and scale the next wall on the list. They knew from observation that the Crawleys spent most evenings in the large shed they had had built within the walled garden. The Americans had heard a local joiner boast of the quality of craftsmanship which had gone into the build to achieve the necessary sound proofing specified by the Crawleys. According to local gossip it appeared that they had built a recording studio in their garden and spent most evenings making music together and recording it for posterity.

This Tuesday evening was no exception and Lance noticed with relief that the light was on in the recording studio once more, leaving the house empty for him to search. He found the back door unlocked and slipped into the deserted home. It was smaller than either of the manses and he was able to confirm relatively quickly that there was not a trace of the isotope present within it. He was disappointed and headed out the back door. The only part of the property which he hadn't been able to test was the shed and he moved over towards it noiselessly. From one of the many pockets of his jacket he took a listening device which he stuck to the corner of the frosted glass window. He put the earpiece in place and listened in to what he had expected would be music or a discussion of recent recordings.

Instead what he heard was quite different. It sounded as if Mrs Crawley was thrashing her husband with some sort of implement while threatening him with more of the same if he didn't mend his ways. He was squealing and taunting her alternately. Unable to resist the temptation he went round the building to the side which had the door and pushed a small camera through the keyhole. The picture was transmitted to a heads up display on his goggles and he found himself staring at what looked like the inside of a dungeon, complete with chains and a whipping post. Mr Crawley was naked and had been tied to the whipping post using velvet restraints. Mrs Crawley was standing behind him wearing a leather bikini and six inch high stiletto boots also made of shiny black leather. She wore matching gloves and in her hands held a massive bunch of nettles. She was flaying her husband with it and calling him every name under the sun. His back was a red mass but he was still taunting her as she whipped him. Lance had seen a lot of things in his life but this was not what he expected to find in a garden shed in a small Borders village.

"Still, each to his own," he thought with a shrug of his shoulders and replaced the camera probe with the sensor from the Geiger counter. The metre didn't move. "Bugger," he thought, "another blank." He was about to head back to the garden wall but couldn't resist one last look at the scene inside. Mr Crawley was now sobbing and pleading for his wife's forgiveness. From the angle of her stance and the way she was holding the bundle of nettles it might be a while before that was forthcoming. Another bout of whipping confirmed his suspicion and Lance headed off reluctantly to the back wall where he sent the necessary signal to bring Steve and the transport back to the drop off point.

"Don't even ask," he said to Steve and gave him the thumbs down again.

Steve shrugged and headed off to Clive's house feeling his mood tailing away with each unsuccessful search. On the bright side, there had been no indication yet of anyone raising the alarm. This was, however, little compensation to the pair as they had started the evening with high hopes of early success and a sharp exit towards London and onward flights to sunnier climes. Still, there were three possible houses remaining and such was the confidence they placed in their intelligence and observations that they were still sure they would track down the money before the night was through.

Steve headed round the two corners that brought them to Clive's house. It was a relatively modern house which had been built twenty years before on a building plot created by the felling of an old dairy wood. With no wall to hide his movements Lance was forced to take a different approach for the search here. Slipping out the side door of the vehicle as before he made his way to the side of the property to where the electricity cable met the house. He took a cable and weight arrangement from one of his jacket pockets and threw the contraption over the cable. The weight went neatly over the power line and dropped within reach of Lance. He grabbed it and started pulling the ends of what was actually a saw-cable up and down till the line broke with a shower of sparks. Every light in the property went out and Lance popped the night goggles on his head. At the same time as he was doing this, Steve casually shot the bulbs on the two street lights which provided light in the area of the house with his silenced pistol, leaving the property in complete darkness.

Lance moved to the back corner of the building and turned his face and goggles towards the large rear window of the lounge. He was unable to see anyone inside the house. He steadied himself, ready to force the back door and burst in. Clive's wife would be at the Women's Rural meeting with David's wife and both husbands would have settled their respective young children into bed by now. The Americans had decided that if they had been unsuccessful by this stage of the search then it would be justified to use force to subdue both Clive and, if necessary, David thereafter at his house nearby. Time was getting on and they had expected the alarm might have been raised by now. Although there had been no sign of the police or other commotion at the previous houses Lance was sticking to plan A and prepared the cosh in his right hand ready to knock Clive out. He wasn't sure how the mild mannered office worker would come to terms with such violence but he figured that was his look-out. However, just as he was about to move to the back door it burst open and Clive and David barrelled through it, knocking lumps out of each other.

"You lying, ungrateful bastard," screamed David as he rolled over the patio and onto the grass, his hands on Clive's throat.

"It's fuck all to do with you. You're just jealous that I found something worth finding instead of all that shit you dug up," replied Clive as he wrestled himself free and swung a kick at David's groin.

David jumped back and avoided it then ran at Clive and they disappeared into the flower bed at the right hand side of Clive's lawn.

Lance stared after them.

"There must be something in the water here," he thought to himself, then quickly slipped into the house through the back door. Once inside he made a quick tour of the building, taking readings with the Geiger counter as he went. He had to be very careful as he checked out the children's bedrooms. The last thing he needed was one of them asking for a glass of water or a bedtime story. Again there wasn't a single reading to suggest the money had been anywhere near Clive's home. He made his way quietly to the back door again, all the time ready with the cosh to subdue any attempted intervention. He needn't have worried. From the rhubarb patch near the bottom of the garden he could hear the unmistakable sounds of the fight continuing between David and Clive.

There was a stream of swearing as one or other of them landed in a large rose bush.

He quickly made his way to the people-carrier which was parked in a lane to the side of Dairy Wood. He startled Steve by appearing at the driver's window and put his fingers to his lips before again giving the thumbs down sign.

"Did you have to thump him?" Steve whispered.

"No, someone else did it for me. I'll tell you later but I know the next house is free so I'm going to leg it down there on foot while the coast is clear. You head off to the next pick-up point and I'll meet you there."

More than a little confused, Steve headed off as instructed.

Lance started making his way to David's house via a series of adjoining gardens. With David definitely fully occupied in Clive's back garden he decided to make the most of the opportunity. He had just vaulted over the fence of David's neighbour's garden and was about to sprint across the lawn when he was aware of a sudden sharp pain in his left ankle. Looking down he saw the smallest dog he could remember seeing in his life. He recognised it as a Jack Russell and it had sunk its teeth into his leg. He shook his leg in a kicking motion but it somehow held fast. The pain was intense. He swiped at it with his hand and it let go.

"Shit," swore Lance as he felt blood trickle down his sock. He was about to start across the garden when the dog clamped its teeth into his other leg at a similar height.

"Would you fuck off," he swore and swipe at it again. The dog let go momentarily and Lance reached for his cosh. Before he could get a good grip of it though the dog had vaulted off a neighbouring wall and sank its teeth into Lance's hand. He dropped the cosh in pain and shook the dog off, catching it with a blow as it fell. Just as he was about to finish it off he heard a slight grunt and looked up to see an Alsatian leaping at him. He could do nothing about it and he fell backwards as it closed its jaws round his right shoulder. He reached for the small knife attached to his belt and was about to use it on the bigger dog when he felt a small but very powerful set of teeth bite into his groin. Although he had been caught out by the bigger dog's attack he now found the strength to break free from both it and the Jack Russell, and with a huge effort and with the knife waving wildly in front of him, he managed to scramble free and make it to the far side of the garden. Once there he leapt over the fence and into David's garden, but not before both dogs had connected again. The Jack

Russell would have been carried over the fence along with Lance if it had not been brushed off his backside by an overhanging branch.

On the other side of the fence Lance crouched with the knife in his hand, ready to kill anything which tried to follow him over. The dogs, however, must have decided their work was done now that the invasion of their own garden had ended and they trotted back to the neighbour's house with their tails wagging in time. After a full five minutes Lance satisfied himself that he was safe in David's garden and assessed the damage done by the dogs. His ankles were both sore and bleeding, as was his shoulder, which had sustained a very painful wound. His bottom was sore but was nothing compared to the pain in his groin. Checking to confirm that David's house was still quiet he dropped his trousers to inspect the damage, just as the owner of both dogs, a retired school teacher called Nessie Jones, looked out of her upstairs window to see what had upset her pets. As she looked out she caught sight of a large man standing in her neighbour's garden drop his trousers and start to touch his groin. In panic mode she dialled 999 to report the first flasher in Kirkton's history.

Lance found to his surprise that he was not bleeding from either the front or the back of his nether regions and pulled his trousers back up. Still in considerable pain he limped over to David's back door and found it locked. He was low on both time and patience by now and took a silenced pistol out of its holster on his thigh. He shot the lock from the door and rushed inside, still holding the gun in his hand. Despite the pain he moved methodically around the house checking the screen for any positive readings. He cursed when yet again there were none. He made his way to the back door and sent the three click signal to Steve. The black people-carrier sped to the rear of the property and, ignoring the bright street light, parked where Lance could make a quick dash into the side door.

Steve could see Lance was struggling to scale the wall and was limping badly. As Lance climbed in he gave the thumbs down sign and Steve drove away.

"I take it that guy David appeared and put up a bit of a fight?" Steve asked.

"I don't want to talk about it but I'll tell you this, you're doing the final one. I've had enough for one night."

"If you're sure. You realise the money must be in that big fellow's farmhouse? I thought you might quite enjoy sorting him out if he gets nosey."

"Under normal circumstances yes," replied Lance. "But the way things have gone tonight I'll let you have the pleasure."

Steve just shrugged as usual and headed out of town towards a back road which skirted round Barry the Gamekeeper's farmhouse. An earlier recce had suggested the best way of approaching the house was through a wooded area to the rear of the farmyard. A small farm road conveniently ran past the wood, allowing the vehicle to be parked well off the main road and for the Americans to approach, hopefully without being seen. Steve stopped the people-carrier and switched off the lights. He had already removed the bulbs from the courtesy lights and opened the door as quietly as possible, getting out to stretch his legs. He opened the side door and stared at Lance as best he could in the darkness. He popped his night vision goggles on and looked closely at his friend. Lance had his trousers round his ankles and was bandaging wounds on both legs. A large padded bandage had already been stuck to his shoulder and an ice pack from the fridge compartment was resting on his crotch.

"This had better be worth it," he said to Steve with an expression of pain as he dabbed disinfectant onto one of the wounds.

"What happened to you?" Steve asked.

"It has been a more eventful night than I anticipated, and we still haven't found the money yet."

"Don't worry, this guy Barry must have it. George said he saw him pay cash for the truck. Almost ten thousand pounds in used notes. If we don't get a reading as soon as we're inside I'll eat my hat."

"You better be right or I'm going to have a word with this Brad fella in London, CIA or no CIA."

Chapter 30

Last House

On balance, they had decided on the way over that they would both go to Barry's farmhouse. If their information was correct then the money must be there. If Barry had a couple of million dollars and pounds in cash in the house he was just the kind to fight to keep it. Steve would go in and Lance would keep watch. Both would wear night vision goggles and carry their pistols. If they found the cash and Barry put up a fight they would ignore Brad's instructions not to hurt anyone. Hurting Barry didn't really count and Brad would understand if he had met him.

Once Lance had finished bandaging himself and taken a couple of pain-killers they got themselves ready. With Steve leading in the centre of the woods and Lance trailing some distance behind him on the left they made their way towards the farmhouse which was in complete darkness. They both felt better about this mission. Armed, working together and fully kitted up, prepared to take out any opposition. This was how they had worked so often in the past.

From the opposite side of the back road, Barry had watched the Americans arrive. He watched them park up and prepare for what looked like an armed assault on his house. So that bitch Donna had persuaded them to get rid of him? He would soon see about that. Fortunately he had been out deer stalking and although he had not managed to find any this time out he had his rifle with him and twenty rounds of ammunition, and now providence had provided bigger game than the odd fallow or roe deer he was used to.

As soon as Lance and Steve had started towards his farmhouse, Barry quickly crossed the road, hidden from view by the people-carrier. He levelled the rifle with its night scope on top of the bonnet of the vehicle and picked out Steve and Lance as they headed towards his house. Both had pistols in their hands, making it clear they weren't intending to pop in for a cup of tea and a chat. So Donna had brought in a couple of hit men to get rid of him, had she, he thought to himself. "Well, they are not going to get me tonight."

Steve and Lance were making good progress through the woods. With the night goggles on it might as well have been daylight. They both hoped that the absence of lights in the building meant that Barry was having an early night and they could catch him unawares. Steve laughed to himself, "so much for civvies in camouflage kit."

It came as a complete shock, therefore, when he felt a thump on his back and slumped forward, realising he had been shot. He cried out in pain and Lance crouched down for protection swivelling his pistol from side to side as he searched for a source of the gun shot. Finding none he crawled over to Steve who was lying on his side gasping for breath.

"I've been shot in the back," he whispered to Lance.

Lance immediately turned towards the direction of the road and tried to pick out any clue of where their assailant could be. He could see no indication through the goggles, nor when he took them off and peered through the darkness. He pulled a first field dressing from his jacket pocket, opened it and placed it over the wound on Steve's back.

"You stay here and I'll get the son of a bitch," he whispered to his friend.

Lance crawled carefully away from Steve through the ferns and undergrowth and worked his way over to the opposite side of the woods from his earlier movement. Staying as low as he could he made his way towards the parked vehicle as quietly as possible. Every few minutes he would stop and listen, looking all the time through the night vision goggles for any sign of whoever was out there. It could be Barry who had somehow got wind of their intentions and laid in wait. It could be any one of a number of people he and Steve had upset over the years. It could even be that Brad guy who had sent them here in the first place. Whoever it was appeared to know what they were doing and had the weaponry to take both of them out. That suggested the last of the options he had considered: Brad or someone else within The Firm had given orders to eliminate the two freelancers while they were in the middle of nowhere. Maybe the whole missing money story had been a ruse from start to finish. At this precise time, though, it didn't much matter to Lance. His friend had been badly, probably fatally, wounded and it was reasonable to assume that whoever had done it was still in the woods and wanted to do the same to Lance. "Well, they are not going to get me tonight," he decided and pressed forward.

Barry had watched the first American fall. He was sure it was the taller one who had needled him at the Wagon. "Good," he thought. "One down, one to go." The other had dropped out of sight immediately and probably gone to check whether his buddy was dead or not. Now there was no obvious trace of him, so it was reasonable to assume that the remaining soldier's training had kicked in and he was even now trying to work back and shoot Barry. He lifted the rifle gently off the bonnet of the vehicle and crept back across the road, intending to move as far back into the trees at the other side as he could. As he reached the other side of the road he tripped on a pothole, landing heavily on his head and accidently firing the rifle as he fell. Stunned, he lay on the road near the front wheels and struggled to get his bearings again. After five minutes or so he managed to recover the strength to crawl into the woods away from his house. When he had crawled a good fifty feet or so but could still see the outline of the people-carrier he slid backwards into the undergrowth and waited. It was unlikely that the other American would simply walk across the road and into his sights and if he had a thermal imaging device with him there was a risk that he could spot Barry in the foliage before Barry saw him. Either way, the American could work his way around to the rear of where Barry was lying in wait - a danger he decided not to risk. If he could keep the engine of the vehicle between him and the remaining American he should be able to hide from any such device. It was a dangerous judgement call but he couldn't just sit while an ex-member of the US special forces got the drop on him.

Lance moved back towards the road as quietly as possible, scanning the area ahead with his night goggles as he went. There was still no sign of life in front of him.

He estimated the first shot had been fired from about two hundred metres away, judging by the sound. In the darkness of the wood that suggested the use of a night scope of some kind and reinforced his suspicion that he and Steve were being targeted by a professional. He had to assume, therefore, that his assailant could see as well as Lance could see, if not better. Perhaps the sniper had a thermal imaging device. If so there was no point simply hiding behind trees and bushes. He had to stay below the level of the ground in front or shield his own image somehow. When a second shot rang out he sunk to his belly and froze. The shot had come from the area of the vehicle. He pulled a handheld thermal imager from one of his pockets and scanned the area. If someone was there he should be able to pick them out. He looked at the people-carrier and realised it was still hot from the night's activities. The shot had definitely come from the other side of the road, suggesting his opponent was using the engine as a shield. Two can play at that game, he thought. As long as he kept the hot engine between him and the shooter he could disguise his whereabouts too. Taking advantage of a deep drainage channel running towards the road he crept over till he was beside the front tyres. Slowly he stood up and scanned the road and the woods at the other side. Again he saw nothing.

"Oh, this guy's good," he thought to himself. He crouched down again in the shelter of the engine's heat. "Now what?" Lance was still limping from his earlier encounters with Nessie Jones' dogs and the bite to his shoulder was more than just sore; damage had been done to his muscles which made any movement agony and some angles of his arm impossible. Although the wound to his groin was not life-threatening, it was a constant distraction to his concentration. In the back of his mind he knew he had to finish this off quickly to give Steve any chance of survival, assuming he was still alive.

The second shot had been fired from very close to the vehicle. Lance reckoned it had been designed to frightening him out of his hiding place at the time. It showed confidence on the part of his opponent, as if he knew he held the upper hand. Had he wanted Lance to make for the people-carrier? If so he had fallen for it, but as yet there was no follow up action. Perhaps it had been a diversion in order to work back towards Steve and either finish him off or get him to talk. Lance wasn't sure what he would want Steve to say, as they had been involved in so many shady activities over the years, either together or separately. He decided on balance to try to work his way back to Steve.

Barry was lying in a clump of nettles which had stung his hands and his face when he had settled into the undergrowth. He had been stung a million times over the years but had never really got used to it. This time it was specifically the fault of the two Americans. His head still hurt and there was a ringing in his ears as if he had mild concussion. He had twisted his ankle as he tried to move off the road after the fall and had a variety of scratches and scrapes from crawling around. Overall then he was sore and angry. There had been no sign of the second American and no sound from the one he had shot. He had to assume that the remaining one had equipment to see Barry at night and would find him sooner or later. If there was going to be a gun fight, he thought to himself, it would be better for him if it was at the OK Corral; or more accurately at his farmhouse, where he could use his knowledge of the layout to his own advantage. Ignoring the various sources of pain he crawled round in a wide semi-circle until he was able to cross the road a good 400 yards from the people-carrier. He ran quickly across to reduce the chance of being spotted, and then half crawled, half ran along a narrow path to the far side of the farmhouse. There he went quickly through his dilapidated garden fence and in through the front door of the house, locking the door behind him. He made his way to the kitchen and grabbed his shotgun and a handful of cartridges to increase his fire power if it came to a shootout.

Lance made it back to where Steve was lying and a quick check informed him that the shot had been fatal. He cursed and took Steve's pistol from his hand.

"You won't be needing that now, old friend," he whispered, with only the slightest hint of affection in his voice. "Don't you worry though; I'll get even with this son of a bitch and take the money off our gamekeeper friend at the same time."

Lance looked towards the farmhouse and steadied himself. The money had to be there and Lance was going to get it and get out with it, whoever was after him. He hadn't been bitten, shot at and watched his friend die for nothing. If the gunman knew why they were here the chances were that he would be at, or covering, the building. He headed towards the farmyard with a pistol in each hand and his night vision goggles on to give him the best view in the pitch dark. If someone was waiting for him in the compound he was prepared to meet them on equal terms and fight it out to the death.

Barry looked out of his bedroom window on the first floor of the farmhouse. He was still struggling to focus on the view but was focussed enough on the danger out there. He was in pain and a little dizzy from his fall but he was home and prepared to defend it against all comers, especially those comers who had defiled poor wee Donna. Through the night scope of his rifle he noticed a shadow move near the back gate to the farmyard. "So there you are," he thought to himself and gently lifted the sash window. Kneeling down he raised the rifle and pointed it towards the area where the movement had occurred. "Just let me see a bit of you," he whispered.

Lance had made it to the shadows of the farm courtyard, still limping but masking the pain with his determination. Whoever was after them would be in the house by now he reckoned. The money had to be here too, if it had ever existed. Either way, he was going in to end this and get even for Steve's death. There was a short gap between the outside edge of the barn where he was standing and the next bit of cover behind a wall marking the start of the garden. He took a deep breath, gritted his teeth and launched himself towards the wall. Half way there he felt a sharp pain in his good shoulder and simultaneously heard a rifle shot from the upstairs window facing the yard. Despite the searing pain he made it to the safety of the wall and lay flat. There he inspected the wound on his shoulder. The bullet had gone in below the clavicle and embedded itself in his shoulder blade. The damage was severe and he struggled to move his arm at all. When he did, the pain was excruciating. There was also a steady stream of blood dripping down his arm and he could feel himself getting dizzy from the blood loss.

Barry was sure he had hit the American but saw him keep moving towards the garden wall. That meant he was probably wounded but still very much alive. When there was no movement for a full five minutes he decided the best plan of attack was to go downstairs and round the house via the front door. That way he could sneak up on his opponent from behind. He crawled away from the window and stood up when he reached the top of the stairs. As he did so his twisted ankle gave way and he tumbled down the stairs head over heels. Half way down the shotgun fired and took a chunk of plaster out of the ceiling.

Outside, Lance heard the shot. "That's him finishing off Barry," he thought to himself. "This guy's a cold bastard right enough; no witnesses."

At the bottom of the stairs Barry picked himself up and looked at the hole in the plasterwork. "Bugger," he thought. "That'll need fixed now."

With a decided limp Barry made his way out of the front door and started working his way round the buildings towards the woods at the rear. He was in considerable pain now and was sweating heavily. He made it to the back gate close to where he had shot Lance. From there he knew there was about thirty feet to the garden wall. With the rifle it would be an easy shot if he had time to aim. If the other American was ready to shoot him, anticipating his movements, he would probably be beaten to the draw. Maybe the shotgun would be a better option. It was easier to aim and would scatter shot in the general direction of his aim. At thirty feet the shot would still be tight enough to incapacitate his opponent and he could then finish him off with either weapon.

Lance heard a scrape on the ground from the direction of the rear gate and turned with both pistols raised. The pain almost made him black out but the adrenalin flowing through his body kept him conscious, just. There was nothing in sight but it was enough to scare him into jumping over the wall and taking a firing position behind it, both pistols resting on the stones for accuracy and to ease the pain. He waited, staring at the gap between buildings which he now knew led to the rear gate.

Barry knew that Lance had jumped the wall from the faint scrambling noise and the involuntary grunt of pain as he landed on the far side. He also knew that meant his direction of approach had been discovered and that the American was probably waiting for him to appear round the corner of the building. He pulled himself back as quietly as he could and went through the rear gate once again. He had a trick or two up his sleeve yet. He continued in the direction away from the gate and house till he reached a dilapidated door in the external wall of the old barn. He stooped and picked up an old rusty key from under a stone beside it and unlocked the door, praying all the time that it would turn silently. He breathed a sigh of relief as the lock turned and he was able to make his way through the doorway and into the building. Stepping carefully on his injured foot he made his way across the floor of the barn and across to the door at the other side. It was slightly open and he could see out of it and across to the side of the garden wall. In the faint moonlight he could just make out the outline of two pistols resting on the top and behind them the outline of a head peering through the sights. "Got you now," he thought to himself.

Lance stared intently ahead waiting for the chance of a shot at his adversary. He was completely alert now, knowing his life depended on it. Whoever had killed Steve and Barry was a cold blooded killer in his own mould or worse and knew their stuff. If he dropped his game for a second he was finished. After an age he suddenly heard a movement to his left from one of the outbuildings and spun round to see a dark figure rush out of a nearby barn with a shotgun in front of him. Lance loosed off two quick shots from the pistols but was not quite quick or accurate enough. He was thrown backwards as both barrels of the shotgun were fired and hit him in rapid succession. He fell onto his back, completely unable to move. Both pistols had fallen from his hands and this time he could not move to pick them up.

"Who are you?" he managed to gasp, but as Barry approached the question was answered for him. "You! Shit! The fat gamekeeper."

It was a bad choice of last words as Barry reloaded and fired both barrels again.

It was a busy night after that for Barry. Had anyone lived close enough to his farm to hear the noise they might have wondered that he chose the early hours of a Wednesday morning to do some digging with his JCB. But nobody lived for miles in any direction. The next day had anyone visited Barry for any reason they would have found the farm looking remarkably similar to before. The only slight change had been an extension to Barry's huge muck heap at the side of the farmyard. This appeared to have stretched to one side by about ten feet, and had they measured it previously they would have found that it was a few inches lower all round where dung had been taken from the top to cover the new area. Barry would have simply moved the whole thing over to one side but he couldn't risk leaving any of the other bodies uncovered.

Chapter 31

Aftermath

Old Bill got the message about the flasher thirty minutes after the local station had received the report. Both duty police officers had been unable to deal with it due to one of the frequent road traffic accidents on a country road the opposite side of Kelso from Kirkton. As usual it involved a newly qualified young driver, and fortunately for all concerned nobody had been seriously hurt. Despite prompt action to get the road clear and traffic flowing again, Bill's colleagues could not avoid a short delay in informing him of the incident in his patch. They knew he liked to hear straight away about anything happening in or around Kirkton. With retirement only a few weeks away, Bill didn't want any problems unresolved in the closing days of his career.

When he heard about the flasher and realised who had reported it he felt obliged to put his uniform back on and visit Nessie Jones in person. Technically he was off duty and it should have been WPC Janice who attended but she had been delayed at the scene of the car crash and Bill knew from bitter experience that any delay in answering Nessie's call outs would result in a complaint; a complaint which Bill would have to deal with when he was next on duty. Better to head that possibility off at the pass.

As he walked the short distance to Nessie's house he began to speculate on who would do such a thing in Kirkton and, having made the decision to expose themselves, why choose Nessie? He couldn't recall any such incident here before and he had only once had to track down a flasher during his time in the Northern Constabulary. That had been a drunk dropping his trousers at a passing tourist in Wick. Hardly a major offence; after all, there wasn't much else to do in Wick after the pubs shut. At the time the sheriff had taken a similar view and admonished the youth who had no previous convictions. He'd had a few since, Bill had noted, but not for flashing. Kirkton wasn't really the type of place you would expect such a crime. People knew each other and looked out for each other. Anonymity in such a crime would be difficult. Either somebody walking their dog would see something, or the victim would recognise the exposed area from memory or reputation. No, it was more likely that Nessie had mistaken what she had actually witnessed. A large man dropping his trousers and waving his private parts about in David Archibald's garden was very unlikely. David himself was immediately ruled out on height. Still, he didn't want any loose ends when he retired. None at all, and this would have to be investigated and resolved quickly as a result.

He would placate Nessie and hand the details to Janice in the morning. She might even recognise the flasher's description he laughed to himself, although on reflection he knew she took her duties too seriously to misbehave in her own patch.

By the time Old Bill made it to work the next day there were a string of reports of incidents in Kirkton needing followed up. He wasn't happy about that at all. After ten years, where a stolen bicycle and cheating in the annual vegetable competition were the criminal highlights, he didn't need a crime epidemic just before he retired. Leafing through the reports of forced entry, footprints on flowerbeds and the noise from a fight between two normally respectable members of the community he sighed deeply. It hadn't even been a full moon he realised, checking the calendar on his desk just to make sure. To cap it all an abandoned black people-carrier had been found burnt out in a layby on the main 'A' road south, which sadly still counted as his patch by just under fifty feet.

"Bugger," was all he could manage as he poured himself the first of what he knew would be many strong coffees that day.

Chapter 32

The President keeps his promise

Brad Dexter entered the White House with a sense of pride. Not at the building or indeed the office of President of The United States. No, he took that stuff for granted. His sense of pride was centred entirely on his own success in obtaining the British passports and driving licences which the commander-in-chief had requested. Boy was he good, he thought. He had been summoned to the White House by phone call from the deputy chief of staff. He had flown back from London personally carrying the documents and had high hopes of actually meeting the President himself. Why else would he be asked to deliver them personally? He went through the rigid security checks along with two military attaches from Canada, a teacher from Wisconsin and her star six year old pupil who had written to President Thackery asking for world peace for her birthday, and a talking dog which was big on 'The US has talented animals' at the time. It was a strange mix of photo opportunities and secret emissaries he thought to himself. Mostly though, he resented arriving at the same time as the dog. Surely he wouldn't have to wait till after the president had posed with it for the assembled media?

Once through security, he was met by a young aide who was waiting for him and ushered him into a side room. "I am Neil Jobson. Thank you for delivering these items personally," the young man began. "The President is very grateful for your efforts in obtaining them. May I have them, please?"

Brad paused, not keen to hand them to anyone but the President himself or, at a real push, to his chief of staff.

"Well I was told to bring them here for the President," said Brad. "I don't..."

"I have been asked to make sure he gets them, Mr Dexter," countered the young man.

"Well I suppose..."

"Surely you didn't expect the President to come and collect them personally did you? He's a very busy man."

Brad was about to make a quip about the talking dog when he thought better of it and handed over the envelope he had brought with him.

"Thank you, Mr Dexter. I am authorised to tell you that the President has mentioned your endeavours on his behalf at his weekly briefing with the director of The Central Intelligence Agency. I'll show you out."

With that Brad was ushered out through the security screen exactly eight minutes after he had passed going the other way. Somewhat deflated, he wandered out into the daylight and thought, "now what?"

Meanwhile the young man did not in fact take the documents to the President, but left the building by a separate exit and climbed into a waiting car.

"Joint Base Andrews," he said to the driver. "No rush, it's nothing urgent." The journey gave him the opportunity to catch up with his girlfriend via his mobile phone without interruptions and he was keen to make it last.

At what most people still referred to as Andrew's Air Force Base, Dr Khalid and his family waited in the VIP reception area looking as bemused as their hosts. They had arrived that day from Baghdad on an overnight military flight with senior forces and diplomatic personnel. They had been treated politely and fed well, but there had been little understanding of why they were there. On arrival at Andrews though, they were met by a presidential aide who took them quickly through security and into the VIP area without any checks of ID or baggage. There, they were offered food and drink. Although they stuck to soft drinks they ate a healthy meal from the buffet. Thereafter there had been an embarrassing pause in proceedings while the aide ran out of small talk and Dr Khalid and his family wondered how long they would be in America. Nobody had confirmed what was happening in the long term, although they were relieved to be out of their own country. A relief strongly tinged with sadness. The aide who met them was as junior as was possible and had no idea what was happening, beyond the fact that he had to meet and greet a family from Iraq who were there as the personal guests of the President.

After what had seemed a very long wait, Neil Jobson arrived and relieved his junior colleague who politely said goodbye and left at a trot.

"Dr Khalid, it is a pleasure to meet you. I am afraid the President was unable to come here personally today to welcome you to the United States; he had some very pressing business to attend to."

Neil, too, thought about the talking dog.

"He has, however, asked me to meet you and provide you with the identity documents for your new life in England. I assume we cannot persuade you to stay here in our fine country?"

"I appreciate all your President has done for me and my family, but our heart is set on a new start in Great Britain."

"Very well then, here are your passports and driving licences where appropriate. You will be our guests here tonight in the accommodation and then tomorrow you will fly to England on a diplomatic flight. Once there we will arrange for you to be taken from the airfield to a lovely town called Swindon where a house been rented for you for a three year period. The President has arranged for you to receive the pension equivalent to a retired army captain which should allow you to get established. Thereafter, it is over to you to move forward."

"And the British are happy with the arrangement?" asked Dr Khalid.

"These passports are the real thing, Dr Khalid, they were authorised in England at the very top."

Neil smiled his best smile and Dr Khalid relaxed.

"Please thank your President from the bottom of my heart. I cannot thank him enough for what he has done for me and my family. Also tell him to get more sleep. He looked very tired when I saw him on television last night. I could recommend some medication which would help."

"I will pass that on, although I am sure his own doctor is on the case."

Neil shook hands with the entire group individually, smiling with each as he did so. He then indicated for an orderly to escort them to their accommodation for their one and only night in the land of the free. As they headed off, still waving and smiling back, he headed over to the reception desk and spoke to the colleague who was standing there waiting to be briefed.

"That's the joker I phoned you about who turned down a new life here for one in England. Look after him and his family tonight and we'll get rid of them tomorrow. I have never seen the President as pissed off as he was with that guy, ungrateful son of a bitch. Goodnight."

Chapter 33

Old Bill's Retirement

A special meeting of the community council was held to say a very fond farewell to Kirkton's very own Sergeant William Borthwick. Although never officially the community policeman for the village, he had always been seen as such by its residents, much to the annoyance of PC Janice Mackay who felt her own efforts went unrecognised as a result.

A large turnout of the great and the good from the village and surrounding farms was swelled by a large turnout of the less great, less good and downright dodgy who all shared a respect for Bill's old-fashioned approach to keeping them safe. He had worn his dress uniform for the occasion, even though technically his retirement had commenced two days before the meeting. His wife had managed to build up her health to the point where she could join him on this important evening.

Henry Parker was master of ceremonies as ever and a number of the ladies of the village had been baking for days in advance, producing a banquet of goodies for everyone to enjoy. The village shop and the two hotels had combined to provide wine and beer at cost price or less, with the community council thus managing to cover the cost of this free bar.

Robbie Buchanan had decided to give up his quest for the missing millions. If it was still in the village it was too well hidden for him to discover. He noticed even the Americans appeared to have given up and left town. Although his contact in London had warned him his expenses would no longer be covered by the department, Robbie had decided to stay on a few days at his own expense in order to wish Old Bill a long and happy retirement. Bill had helped Robbie with some tit-bits of information, albeit to no effect.

Bill himself was leaving with some regrets but with a lot of relief. There had been a flurry of incidents in the village recently and he regretted not being able to tidy them all up. He had managed to bring an uneasy peace to the lives of David and Clive (with the help of their wives). Nessie had been assured that there would be no repeat of the flasher incident while PC Janice Mackay was on patrol, although he noticed with amusement that Nessie still referred to her as WPC Mackay. A number of houses had taken security advice from Janice and replaced old locks or started using the perfectly serviceable ones which had always been in place. Overall though, he was relieved at retiring while he still had his health and could look forward to many years away from sheltering in draughty doorways on the nightshift.

Henry called for everyone's attention, and as a hush finally settled in the village hall, made a speech which perfectly captured the mood of the village and conveyed the thanks of its inhabitants. At the end of it he presented Mary with an enormous bouquet of flowers and Bill with an engraved crystal whisky decanter with matching glasses along with a twenty five year old bottle of his favourite malt. To finish the formal part of the evening everyone gave three cheers and sang 'for he's a jolly good fellow'.

Bill and Mary circulated round the crowd for the rest of what was a late evening, humbled by the genuine feeling of gratitude from everyone they spoke to. There was also a sadness in the room that Bill and Mary had decided to move away from the village to a warmer climate, but an understanding too that this would be of great benefit to Mary's health.

Bill even found his hand being shaken by people whom he had brought to book over the years who all assured him that there were no hard feelings. He assured them that he would come out of retirement to sort them out again if necessary, and they laughed together as if they were old friends.

People headed off slowly but surely as the hour grew late. Robbie made his way unsteadily towards Betty MacVicar's Bed and Breakfast hoping for one last night of relaxation there before he headed reluctantly home to Kingussie, a place he realised no longer felt like home.

As Bill and Mary said their final farewells and headed for the door, they were met by Billy MacPherson, standing with a glass of coke in his hand.

"It'll no be the same without you," Billy said in all seriousness.

Bill looked him straight in the eye and replied, "Look after it for me please."

"I will," replied Billy.

And with that Old Bill headed home from a community council meeting in Kirkton for the last time.

Chapter 34

A Place in the Sun

Old Bill sat on the sun lounger beside the edge of the Dalmation coast of the Adriatic Sea. The temperature was a pleasant 20 degrees, but then it was autumn. The view was of massive, steeply sloping mountains rising straight from the water across the bay from his house. Some people found themselves developing a feeling of being hemmed in and enclosed when they visited him and his wife Mary, such was the grandeur and scale of the mountains surrounding Donji Stoln. Bill for his part, found it very re-assuring. It was remote enough to feel safe from the world and yet within easy travelling distance was the airport at Tivat, the large and ever growing town of Budva with its nightlife, and Lidls store and all the history anyone could ask for at the medieval city of Kotor.

Bill and Mary had passed through the area in their motorhome five years earlier on a grand tour of Europe which lasted four weeks. After taking a wrong turning returning north from Budva on their way to Dubrovnik,

Bill had found himself struggling to drive the vehicle along the single track road which weaved its way past the various houses along that part of the coast. The cars, taxis and buses coming the other way seemed to give no quarter, while behind him locals were less than impressed with his pace. On several occasions he felt obliged to pull over into a driveway or café car park to let someone past, only to have fingers or fists waved at him. The task of navigating the route was made all the more difficult by the local pedestrians walking in the middle of their road. Squeezing between them, passing vehicles heading the other way and walls on the edge of gardens was tricky. The most difficult part was paying attention to the road when the pedestrians were beautiful young girls in the briefest of bikinis. Bill only just managed to concentrate on these occasions but the views of mountains and girls in bikinis had stayed with him over his final five years as a bobby in the Scottish Borders.

He often managed to get through the coldest of his shifts with thoughts of one day returning to that beautiful coast with its beautiful women. He had even researched the cost of buying a home in the area when he retired but found that Russian buyers had pushed up prices anywhere near Budva beyond the reach of his police pension and savings. Mary was very keen on a sunny retirement, suffering as she did from rheumatism and arthritis, and had enjoyed her grand tour in the caravan so much that almost any of the areas visited would do. As an added bonus to Bill's thoughts on the matter, she was not very keen on sitting directly in the sun in the way he did, opening up the prospect of Bill sitting peacefully alone in the sun getting to know the locals without the constant company of his wife. His thoughts had even drifted to the young women he had failed to avoid staring at as he eased the motorhome along the narrow road whilst simultaneously staring at their bikini clad bottoms. Perhaps he might get to know some of them? Perhaps some of them might find a fine figure of a retired British policeman somehow exotic? Perhaps while his wife hid from the hottest rays of the day he might be invited to their home? Perhaps... perhaps... perhaps. Thus he had survived the coldest wind, rain and snow of the winter shifts as he served his time until retirement.

Now, however he was actually there, in Montenegro, sitting beside the Adriatic and yes, the young women or their daughters and sisters were still walking along the road in bikinis on their way to or from a dip in the water. He too was taking dips in the water and he was getting to know some of the locals. They liked his solid reliability. They liked Mary's home baking and her eagerness to learn local recipes. The locals admired the new neighbours' attempts at learning the language.

Most of all, though, the locals admired Bill's boat. Boat was perhaps an understatement. Large private yacht would be more accurate. He must have been a senior policeman indeed to afford such a beautiful craft as the Mary 2, they reasoned. Fifty two feet of gleaming hull and superstructure with six cabins and a diving platform at the rear, all paid for in cash with US dollars. The local children were soon encouraged to treat the diving platform as a floating playground and took up the offer with glee. Their parents were initially concerned and called them off, but found that Bill was more than happy for them to make full use of it whenever they wished. In turn he became acquainted with a number of young mothers who supervised the children during the day. One in particular seemed to seek out his company rather than the other way around. He gathered the child's father had never returned from the Balkans conflicts of recent years. Whether this was through ill fate or by choice was unclear to Bill. Either way, she was a single mother and seemed lonely.

All in all, his first few months of retirement were going very well and very much according to plan. Wherever the money had come from there was no way it could be traced to him here. Life was good, and he hoped might soon get even better.

Chapter 35

Dame Jennifer ?

Jennifer Allerdyce sat in her office listening to Robbie Buchanan confirm that he had no idea at all where the American's cash had gone after being dropped on Kirkton. Many people appeared to have money to spare. Money appeared regularly for causes when needed. The recently and affluently retired all checked out, as did the village's only apparent lottery winner. He had even befriended the local Bobby before his retiral and struck a blank there too. If anyone would have known it would have been Old Bill, but he had obviously no knowledge of money landing from the gods, nor did his local constabulary colleagues. In short he had turned up nothing, zilch, zippo. He did not elaborate on his new friends or his adventures along the way. Jennifer was interested in results and he had nothing to show. He didn't care. She had forced him into this farce from the beginning and he had resented that. In a way he was pleased he had found nothing. His conscience was clear, having tried his best.

Jennifer seemed to take his news very calmly, but then she was employed to stay calm whatever happened, indeed to remove all emotion from her decision making. While Robbie talked she read and then re-read a single sheet of A4 which had been handed to her during the call. Her face showed no emotion.

"Thank you for your efforts, Robbie," she said and added almost sympathetically, "I hope your leg isn't acting up too much. I mean the missing one. I suggest you head back to Inverbeg or wherever and enjoy retirement again."

Robbie was about to correct her on two accounts; of living in Kingussie and not being as retired as much as he had hoped when she hung up without warning.

Jennifer looked again at the memo in her hand and pressed the intercom to her secretary, John.

"Send Mr Dexter in please, John."

A few seconds later John showed Brad Dexter into Jennifer's office. On Jennifer's specific instructions John stayed in the room taking a seat at the rear wall. Brad looked uncomfortable that John had stayed and, had he noticed, he would have seen that Jennifer was pleased that he felt uncomfortable. Despite this, Brad was his usual obnoxious self and started immediately on his favourite subject of late.

"Any sign of our loose change?" he smiled as he said it, suggesting the money was of no consequence, but she assumed it was or he wouldn't be here. "I've had to protect your ass from a whole lot of flack over this one, sweetheart. I hope you can give me something in return, one way or another."

Jennifer fought the urge to vomit and longed for the days of Brad's predecessor who had been so polite and business-like. A sociopath by all accounts, but much more pleasant to deal with.

"I am happy to say that we have made progress locating your money."

Brad looked disappointed as if he enjoyed the task of "protecting her ass" and may have hoped it would feature somehow in his reward.

"I thought your one-legged friend on the ground had drawn a blank?"

"He did," continued Jennifer. "Fortunately, although we are a small organisation compared to the CIA, we have had other staff on the trail. Here are the details and current whereabouts of the person who found your money, the bank accounts where your money ended up, along with confirmation of some rather large cash purchases he has recently made. He is still a British citizen with a wife in poor health, so we would appreciate it if he could survive your colleagues' repossession visit."

"Don't you worry your sweet tush about him. We can probably get most of it back electronically without anyone dropping by. Emails after that should get him to send back whatever else is recoverable. You know me, Jenny. The soul of discretion."

He smiled what he believed to be a winning smile and Jennifer simply stared back, indicating the interview was at an end. She resented the way he managed to make a reference to her bottom in almost every sentence. It would have been very different if he had been dealing with any of her male predecessors, although most of them might have been as interested in his bottom.

Thanking her again profusely, Brad left.

When he had gone John turned to his boss. "So who was it that found the money?"

"It seems that the local policeman from Kirkton has retired to the Dalmation coast with an unfeasibly large pension fund. I suspect over the next few days this policeman's lot will not be a happy one."

Chapter 36

Conclusion

To say that Swindon had been a disappointment to Dr Khalid and his family would have been something of an understatement. His youngest son had not managed to get a place in the nearest school to their new home and had to travel by bus across most of the town. As a result he began to neglect his studies and started missing school.

Dr Khalid's daughter had failed to gain a foothold in the local artistic set and her husband had secured only basic manual work. Tariq had fallen into bad company while waiting to enter university and there was a considerable danger that he might give up his dream of medicine altogether, preferring a life of recreational drug use instead.

As a result of his concerns, Dr Khalid had decided that his family would tour the length and breadth of the United Kingdom looking for their ideal home. A place where they could all be happy in peace, without any of the dangers or threats they had previously faced. On the return leg of their tour they had taken a wrong turn heading for the A1 and the road south, thus finding themselves in the tiny village of Kirkton. Hungry, and with time getting on, they were relieved to find that the first hotel they tried had vacant rooms and made them feel immediately welcome. The menu was imaginative and the young chef, who introduced himself as Kevin, came through from the kitchen to discuss any special dietary requirements they may have. He seemed genuinely pleased to be asked for something not on the menu and headed for his kitchen to produce what turned out to be one of the best meals the family had eaten since arriving in Britain. The total bill was very reasonable and the locals all seemed very friendly, including the Khalids in the wide ranging conversations and banter on local gossip.

Dr Khalid looked at his wife who seemed to be thinking along the same lines. She believed in fate and perhaps it had been no accident that their satnav had failed them and brought them here. She nodded at her husband, not needing to say anything after so many years of marriage in the most difficult of circumstances. Maybe they could stay for another night to have a look at what accommodation was available locally. None of them was in any rush to get back to Swindon. A few days here walking amongst the hills and beside the rivers and streams might be just what they all needed: a restful break in this peaceful idyll.

Dr Khalid looked round the room to find that Tariq was deep in conversation with the barmaid. She was a pretty girl of generous proportions and seemed to be resting her chest on the counter in line with Tariq's gaze. Dr Khalid was very liberal in his outlook and chuckled to himself.

"Doesn't look like we will meet any resistance there," he whispered to his wife who shushed him with mock embarrassment.

Everyone in the bar of the hotel seemed happy and contented with their life. Everyone that is, except a large figure at a corner table, dressed in camouflage clothes and heavy boots. This figure was scowling and eyed the handsome young stranger at the bar with focused hatred and with resolve.

"Looks like I might have to rearrange my muck heap again," Barry Appleby thought to himself.

<u>George Milne – Cat Detective</u>

George doesn't live his life; it happens to him. That is until his side line scam of pretending to help old ladies find their missing cats brings him to the attention of a brutal drugs boss. From then on he has to decide whether to take charge of his future or risk not having one. An unlikely love affair set against a background of drugs, gang violence, cats and zebra onesies. The ideal read for everyone who loves cats and for those who hate them.

"I'm looking for George Milne, is he in?" asked Jimmy staring unashamedly at the zebra's cleavage.

"Not at the moment," Carol replied. "He's gone out."

"Do you know when he is likely to return?" asked Jimmy managing to look Carol in the eye. Behind Carol another zebra, at least as beautiful as the first, made its way to the kitchen waving at Jimmy as it went followed seconds later by another whose hood was up but whose figure suggested yet another beautiful creature. What the hell has this Milne guy got going for him, he wondered, apart from an unnatural fascination with animals?

<u>Body and Soul</u>

Two very different men are on a pathway to a meeting
which will change both their lives forever. One is a
Scottish ex-soldier, ex-boxer, ex-husband, ex-father and
ex-drunk struggling to turn his life around. The other,
the CEO of an American multi-national, has both wealth
and power. They do not know each other and only the
American believes he knows the true purpose of their
meeting. In fact both have been duped in different ways
and as their lives begin to unravel they must try to deal
with the truth if they can. Only one has the skills and
determination to survive.

*After failing to wake Frank he dragged him into the
shower which conveniently only produced cold water and
turned it on full. The effect wasn't immediate, but slowly
the old fighting, kicking Frank began to re-appear, curse
the first house guest he had had for six months and try to
throw him out. After an initial but futile attempt to
punch Paddy's lights out Frank calmed down enough to
recognise his visitor.*

Made in the USA
Columbia, SC
25 July 2017